Haughty Boys of Ngoroke

IMALI J ABALA

Nsemia

First Edition: August 2015
Published by Nsemia Inc. Publishers (www.nsemia.com);
Oakville, Ontario, Canada

Edited By: Charles Phebih-Agyekum
Cover Concept & Illustration: Robert Maina Kambo
Cover Design: Danielle Pitt
Layout Design: Kemunto Matunda

Note for Librarians:
A cataloguing record for this book is available from Library and Archives Canada.

ISBN: 978-1-926906-44-7

Dedication

In memory of my mother, Joyce Muhonja Abala, my lifelong teacher and source of inspiration.

Acknowledgements

I cannot express enough gratitude to Dr. Juliette Schaefer for her kindness and wisdom on this project and Sister Roberta Miller for her moral support and encouragement. My dearest friend and sister, Ebby S. Luvaga, who is my biggest critic and supporter. Finally, I owe my deepest gratitude to my son Abala, who is always willing to listen to everything I write— Ahsante Baba!

About the Author

Imali J Abala was born in Western Kenya. She currently lives in the United States. She is a professor of English at Ohio Dominican University. Her publications include: *Moody Mood and Red Round Ball* (first book in her Children's Series), *Drum Bits of Terror, A Fallen Citadel* (a collection of poetry), *The Dilemma of Jahenda: The Teenage Mother, The Disinherited and Move on, Trufosa.* Some of her other works have also appeared in the following anthologies: *Out of the Depth: Poetry of Poverty, Courage and Resilience, Anthology of Contemporary Short Stories and Poems from East Africa, A Thousand Voices Rising*, and *Reflections: An Anthology by African Women Poets,* a one-of-a-kind collection of poetry by contemporary African women poets.

Chapter 1

Jared Agoyi pulled a slingshot from his school bag slung over his shoulder and held it in his left hand. He thrust his free hand into his pocket and fished out pellets of rock. Holding the wooden handle of his slingshot, he placed a pellet in its leather pad. He aimed it to his target, pulled the leather strap, and released the pad just as his target, an owl, took flight. He bit his lower lip in disgust for missing it. 'Not to worry,' he thought. 'There are more targets in the vicinity.' A dove flew in his view, and its fate was sealed. Agoyi took aim and pulling the slingshot. Once again, he let it go. The pellet buzzed to its target as it flapped its wings with ease, soaring-up into empty space. 'What a shame!' he exclaimed. He had missed it too, and this caused his heart to sink with disappointment. He resolved that the next target to emerge in his view, he would not miss it, not one bit. He meant it, for there was no room for error. He was determined to point *it* with a razor's precision, being he had only one pellet left. Luckily, he did not have long to wait, for just as his thoughts came to a close, he saw a fleet of geese. He stood at ease and watched the fleet for a while. Their flight was majestic and synchronized in the bright afternoon sun. He watched them in silence until they veered close to in view. He bit his lower lip in excitement. Without thinking, he reached for his last pellet, tightened his grip around the wooden handle of the slingshot, closed his right eye, and took aim as the geese flew in a v-formation. No sooner had he released the pellet than he heard a poof-like-sound as the pellet struck one of the unsuspecting birds. The bird tumbled onto the ground like a rock. Agoyi sprung to his feet to where the bird fell. It was lying on the ground with a gaping hole to its chest. Its wound was covered in blood. Seeing it was fatally injured, he felt some remorse for having destroyed a life, but he had no desire for its carcass; instead, he walked away, heading home. That was one in the afternoon, and Agoyi was on his way home from Bute Primary School.

When Agoyi arrived at their gate, it was a quarter past one in the afternoon. The sun was sizzling hot as its skylights showered the horizon. He halted in his tracks when he saw his stepmother sitting under the jacaranda tree. It was unusual for her to be sitting beneath the tree shade for she was always frightened of crawling bugs. Her back was bent like a bow and it was hard for him to discern what she was doing. Her sight filled him with fright. He moved his eyes away from her and ogled into the sky. The immense cloudless sky seemed to grow wider, receding further away from earth. He lowered his eyes again to steal another peek at her. She was unmoved by his presence at the gate. His half-brother Laban, who was two years his junior, was nowhere in the vicinity. Quickly, he scanned the compound before he made his next move. His eyes zeroed in onto the kitchen. There was no sign of cooking. No smoke emanated from its chimney, none whatsoever. He sighed with disappointment. 'Perhaps she has already cooked lunch,' he thought, but that was further from the truth. Suddenly, he experienced sharp pangs of hunger in his stomach, and that caused him to roll his eyes back to his stepmother, back to the kitchen, and back to her again. She did not notice him at the gate (at least, so he thought); for she was still in the same position she had been since his arrival—a curved bow. He heaved a big sigh again, but it was not a sigh of relief.

As he turned to take his next step, Agoyi took short, timid and calculated steps, almost afraid to disturb the curved bow under the tree shade. He had to make his way to the kitchen to find a morsel to pacify his hunger . . . Though inwardly, he knew what he would find: Nothing. That truth did not stop him from venturing into the almost deserted house. No sooner had he got into the kitchen, than he noticed its strangeness: It was a deserted desert; the fire was out; the stove was cold, and no sign of cooking anywhere. Right away, a segment of gloom overcame him, just like it had many times before. Certainly, he knew it was not going to be last. Nevertheless, this time, it was different! He had had enough and, from his vantage point, enough was enough. He could not stand the abuse any longer! Just then, he recalled the goose he had struck moments ago with nostalgia. Yes, it would have made a perfect lunch. Unfortunately, he had abandoned it to vultures.

As he walked out of the kitchen, his mind seethed with rage, and his stomach churned with hunger. 'What to do! What to do!' he wondered. He stopped right at the doorway, paralyzed with his stepmother's dishes neatly washed and arranged on the dish rack. That made him even angrier. The thought she must have cooked earlier in the day, fed her son Laban, but left nothing for him, nagged him. He rolled his eyes away from the dishes to her. She was sitting under the canopy of the jacaranda tree painting her toenails and still curved like a bow. Untouched! Unmoved! Her indifference caused a jolt of anger to mount within him even more like a bad poison. He felt like an insignificant gnat. He did not move away from the doorway. He just stood there dazed and stupefied. When she raised her head to steal a peek at him, their eyes coincidentally locked. He sized her just as much as she did him. He noticed the coldness in her empty large eyes, but his remained defiant and questioning: 'Why?' She had no answer for him.

Slowly, but surely, Agoyi walked away from the door in her direction. As he approached her, his knees wobbled, but he steadied himself. She looked at him coldly, but Agoyi was ready for confrontation. She beat him to it. Before he could ask her anything, she snapped at him:

"What do you want?"

"I was going to ask about lunch!"

"Stop bothering me you imbecile! Can't you see I am busy?" she barked. Her voice was hard and cold.

"But mo . . ." he protested.

"Did you hear what I said?"

"I was just going to say . . ." but he lost his trend of thought and simply blurted out, "I am really hungry, you . . . you . . . !"

"Go cook if you want, but for the love of peace, leave me alone! I am not your slave!" she yelled.

Flabbergasted, Agoyi looked on, for he had never thought of her as a slave.

"Did you hear me!" she roared.

Agoyi did not move a muscle.

"Get lost, will you!" she yelped.

"You don't even care about me!" Agoyi yelled back.

"Sue me then!" she said as the veins in her neck throbbed dangerously.

He mumbled something about reporting her to his father when he returned.

"You do just that!" she blurted, but he did not pay her any attention.

Defeated, Agoyi walked away towards the main house, his mind still seething with a dangerous anger. For once, he felt the injustice of his life. If only his mother was still alive, it would have made a difference.

As he shuffled his feet to the house, he could feel his stepmother's eyes piercing his back. He did not look back, and she did not move as though fossilized underneath the tree.

As he drew close to the house, he paused, rotated his head, and glimpsed in her direction. She was no longer looking at him. He turned his head away from her and towards the door. He took a couple of steps and stopped right at the entrance. He reached out for the knob, turned it, and pushed the door open. The room was dimly lit. The air inside was not only warm, but also soothing. Yet, the emptiness of the room terrified him, just like the emptiness he felt inside. He was terrified of his hunger. He was terrified of his stepmother's mean spirit. He was terrified of everything. Once again, thoughts of his departed mother flashed his mind. He wished she were still alive, and his stepmother, the devil incarnate, were the dead goose.

"Close the door before the hens come in there to defecate on the floor," she barked.

Agoyi did not heed her. How dare she think about the house when his stomach churned with hunger? . . . Instead of shutting the door, he dropped his bottom on a hard wooden chair and closed his eyes.

"Agoyi wa Givondo close that door this minute or else you are going to be sorry you didn't," she bellowed again.

Agoyi did not like the sound of her voice, so he complied without question. He roughly stood up, walked to the door, and slammed it shut. The door rattled dangerously.

"You piece of crap!" she yelled. Agoyi did not heed her insult.

As he walked back to his chair, something blue caught his eye. He wondered why he had not seen it before. Right there, on the dining table, two twenty shilling notes were awkwardly placed. The sight of the money was enough to make him forget the anger he felt within. His eyes gaped wide and delightfully as a sinister smile formed on his lips. Without thinking, he raced to the table and reached for the money. Afraid of the consequence, his hand froze in the mid air. 'Take the money or starve?' he wondered.

His stomach grumbled a little, just as he was still in contemplation: 'To take or not take the money.' He thought of how a bottle of Crest Bitter Lemon and some *mandazi* would surely pacify his hunger. The money was too tempting for him to resist. He did not put much thought into the consequences of his action save a brief prayer: 'Please God forgive me for what I am about to do!' He quickly grabbed one of the twenty shilling notes, pushed it in his pants pocket and walked out of the house. His stepmother had not moved. She raised her head, giving him a mean look, but he did not care about that.

"Where do you think you are going young man?"

"Out!" he said in an irritated voice.

"Out where?" she added.

Agoyi did not answer. He simply walked out of the compound. At the gate, he turned left towards the main road, the only road that joined the village to civilization. At the junction, he turned right and walked all the way to a nearby *duka,* which was a quarter a mile from home. He bought a bottle of Crest Bitter Lemon and some *mandazi.* He mauled the *mandazi* gluttonously and cleaned his parched throat with several gulps of Bitter Lemon. It was as tasty as he had thought. In four giant gulps, he finished the bottle. Having pacified his hunger, he loitered around the shop for several hours. He met several of his friends before returning home.

When Agoyi returned home that evening, his stepmother was no longer sitting under the jacaranda tree. She was in the kitchen preparing supper, for he could see whiffs of smoke wafting from its chimney. He could also smell the savoury flavours of her cooking, but because he was no longer hungry, he did not pay it any attention.

Without thinking, Agoyi marched and dropped his body onto the ground like a log under the jacaranda tree. As he sat there, his thoughts moved back and forth from his stepmother to his mother. Surely, his real mother would have left him something to eat; perhaps, a hot potato with tea, or cooked bananas, or *ugali* with *mutere*. As these thoughts floated his mind, a whirlwind moved towards the jacaranda, but it spun itself out, and not before fluttering the giant leaves above him. Then, the air was still again. He felt a sense of calm envelop him. He sat dazed in the stillness of the evening, thinking that he would have to be the first person to tell his father what he had done. Yes, he would confess his crime: 'Father, please forgive me! I have committed a terrible crime. I stole my stepmother's twenty shilling note from the table.' I bought food to pacify his hunger. Yes, his admission of his guilt was greater than his denial of it. It was the *right* thing to do.

He closed his eyes to the sound of his stepmother's footsteps as she went about her work. He had to devise a good line to tell his father the *truth*, his admission of guilt. He justified it to himself in this manner: "It was not a moral sin to steal to save a life, *his life*. My father would understand." Even He who was greater than his father would agree. He did not buy *bangi*—weed—with the money. He did not buy *busa*—a local brew—with the money. He did not buy cigarettes with the money. He bought food and thus felt vindicated in his actions. His stepmother was wrong and the guilty party for denying him food.

While he was still lost in thought, he did not hear as his stepmother stole stealthily towards him. Unbeknownst to him, she ambushed him. Startled, he saw her bending over him with a murderess's eyes. Her blood thirsty brown eyes fiercely pierced into his and penetrated deep into his soul. There was no love in them. On her lips, a crooked twisted smile appeared, while in her right hand, she held a sharpened knife. Had the sun been up, sparks of its sharpened edge would have glittered. The veins emerged from her temple to her neck and throbbed dangerously as though they were about to rupture. Agoyi lost all the energy in his body, immobilized by the craze of a madwoman. His feet were useless to him. He did nothing. There wasnothing that he could have done. 'What a strange day!' he thought.

His inaction worsened the situation. As she drew her right hand high up into the air, Agoyi ducked, just as she buried the knife into his upper thigh. She was aiming for the heart, but his instincts saved him. The pain he felt as the knife tore through his flesh was so great that he screamed as loud as he could. He clutched onto his thigh as tightly as he could, but his pain was unstoppable, as his thoughts, once more, took flight to his departed mother. 'Her spirit must have saved me!'

Blood gushed out of his thigh like a stream, soaking his hands. Instead of dislodging the knife out of his flesh, Agoyi's stepmother ran to her doorsteps, yanked the door open, stepped inside, and slammed it shut behind her, leaving him for dead in a pool of his own blood. The door rattled behind her. Agoyi's screams of agony drew neighbours to his home. He could not remember much about what happened after the assault, save for the numerous eyes he saw gawking at him. He did not move! He did not say a word! He simply closed his eyes. In that instant, life had no meaning. . .

Chapter 2

5:30P.M.   Joseph Agivondo, Agoyi's father, arrived home from work to a pandemonium scene right in his compound. That was in December,a week before Christmas. As a middle-aged businessman, about forty-eight years old, he narrowly missed having a heart attack when he saw a strange unfolding drama at his home. He was a sturdy man in appearance with an impeccable smile, clean shaven, and dressed in his navy blue business suit. In his left hand, he carried a black briefcase exuding a posture of utmost importance. Whenever he walked, his head stood above his shoulders and his back ever straight as though steel poles ran down his back. All that compressed mannerism changed when he saw what was happening in his compound, of people running in and out of his house to his jacaranda tree. Surprised, his eyes opened wide and his mouth turned at the corners. Each man and woman in his home wore this worried look. A mere glance at them made him realize all was not well. In panic, he dropped his briefcase right at the gate, not caring about its content and racing to where the crowd was assembled. It was under the shade of his jacaranda tree where a crowd had formed a barricade. He did not even have the presence of mind to ask: "What is going on here?" He simply sprinted towards the horde.

Forcing his way through the barricade, he was horror-stricken to see his son sprawled upon the ground. His body jerked uncontrollably like a fish on a dock. He was lying in a pool of blood with his eyes shut as though he were dying. The upper part of his thigh was tightly tied with a *kanga* which was socked red with blood. This sight made his heart miss a beat. For a split second, he thought he might have lost him the way he had lost the boy's mother. Tearing off his coat and casting it to the side, he bent over the boy; his steel spine was now curved into a bow. Clasping the boy's head between his masculine palms, he ogled into the boy's eyes trying to see if there was any semblance of life still left in him.

"Agoyi," he shouted his name as loud as he could. "Can you hear me?" There was fear in his voice. The boy did not answer. Though the boy could faintly hear his father's terrified voice, he was too feeble to respond.

"Agoyi! Agoyi!" Agivondo's frantic voice persisted as he nudged the boy gently on his side. "Please tell me you are alright!"

Without saying a word, the boy slowly pushed his eyes open. They were pale washed and tired. He pushed them shut again only to reopen them momentarily. The sight of his father bending over him caused fresh tears to form at the corner of his eyes. He felt its warmth as it slowly glided down his cheeks. Above him, countless perfect rings of black gawked at him. He tried to force a smile, but the pain in his thigh throbbed unbearably that he shut his eyes again, gritting his teeth.

"He is alive!" his father exclaimed. "Did you see that? My boy is alive . . . He can hear me. You can hear me son, right?" he queried. Gently, he slid his thumbs down the boy's temples to wipe them dry.

Agoyi nodded in a slow motion.

"You'll be okay," his father said in an assuring tone. "You will be alright!"

Turning to one of his neighbours, he ordered: "Could you please get me that wheelbarrow by the kitchen!"

On Agivondo's command, the man who had been sent sprinted towards the kitchen to fetch the wheelbarrow.

When Agivondo turned to look at his son's face again, the boy had this questioning look. "Why . . . Father?" he heard a weak, broken voice of his son question, "Why?"

Agivondo was at loss. "I don't know son. I simply don't know!" on second thought, he added: "Tell you what, let me take you to Maseno hospital first and after your treatment, I can get to the root cause of all this."

Agivondo did not know what had happened, for he had not probed anyone for the answers behind his son's injury. Anger mounted within him, but he suppressed it. He did not ask about his wife nor look for her. His son's welfare took precedence. And just like his son, tears began to sting the rims of his eyelids. To mask it from his neighbours, he turned his face away from them.

"Why Father?" the boy continued to mumbled again and again.

"Let us not worry about that now son. Everything is going to be alright."

When the man who had gone to get the wheelbarrow returned, Agivondo dashed into his house, grabbed a sisal sack and a blanket and returned to where Agoyi was still laying. He placed the sisal sack on the wheelbarrow and then added the blanket for cushioning.

"Help me get him on the wheelbarrow," Agivondo said, but it was a mute request because a couple of his neighbours were already at work. Bending over the boy, they carefully and gently lifted him off the ground, resting him on the wheelbarrow, and propping his head with the blanket. When certain he was in a comfortable position, Agivondo and two other neighbours wheeled Agoyi away from home to the hospital. The journey to the hospital was rough and bumpy. And with this constant bumpiness of the road, the boy bobbed his wobbly head on the rim of the wheelbarrow. This made the four milestrip even longer.

By the time they arrived at the hospital, the sun had already tumbled into the western hemisphere leaving only a faint glow of light on the horizon. The boy was admitted on the spot. Immediately the nurse on duty took one look at him, she knew she had to attend to him right away, cleaning his bloody wound and leg. Only then did she realize the depth of the lesion. The wound was two inches wide and one inch deep that he needed sutures to sew the edges of the cut together. Luckily, the knife had not penetrated any of the major arteries in his leg, but the boy had lost a lot of blood. He was going to need a blood transfusion.

No sooner had the nurse cleaned his wounds than she inserted an intravenous line into one of his veins to replenish his lost blood. She also gave him a tetanus injection as precautionary against tetanus infection and painkillers to numb his pain. The rest was left for the doctor. After that he dozed off. Nobody probed the boy for what happened. There was plenty of time for that later . . .

Throughout the night, the Nurse came in and out of his room for three reasons: Check on his condition. Take his blood pressure. Take his temperature. Make sure he was not in pain. The rest was left for when the doctor came in the morning.

Chapter 3

Agoyi opened his eyes to the bright rays of the early morning sun. That was around seven fifteen in the morning. He turned his body to face the window. The sun showed its edge above the eucalyptus tree and its blinding rays penetrating deep into his room. The eucalyptus tree was massive, with its branches and towering leaves spreading wide and providing a shade for the security guard hired to watch hospital grounds. The leaves also provided security to uncountable crows that were a nuisance to those at the hospital. Worse still, patients in ward 7, where Agoyi was admitted, found their hooting disheartening. Rumour had it that whenever these birds congregated around the tree, someone died. Their permanence at the hospital spoke volumes. Agoyi watched the crows as they flew in and out of the tree with loud swiftness, reminding of the goose he had killed the previous day. The sight of these creatures depressed him, for there was something dreadful about them. Bright beams of light peered through the eucalyptus leaves to his room. The light was so intense he had to turn again away from it, facing the half-closed door that led to the main ward. There was nothing there to see. He moved his eyes away from the door to his right. His father was slouched in a wooden chair with his head leaning on its back and tilted to the side. His arms awkwardly rested on his thighs, but his eyes remained closed. His hair was unkempt; his shirt was wrinkled; and it was the shirt he had worn the previous morning.

Sensing his son was awake, Agivondo, who was drowsy

with sleep, moved, shifting his weight on the chair, but remained soundless. Similarly, Agoyi moved; this time face-up ogling into the ceiling.

"Agoyi," Agivondo said, a faint smile appearing at the corners of his mouth.

"Yes father!"

"How are you feeling this morning?"

"Much better than yesterday."

"Would you like something to eat?" Agoyi did not answer.

"Are you hungry?" Agivondo rephrased his question.

It was only then that Agoyi remembered he had not eaten a decent meal save for the *mandazi,* which had gotten him in trouble with his stepmother.

"Would you like something to eat?"

"Yes please!"

"What would you like?"

Several of Agoyi's favourite meals flashed his mind— *ugali* with chicken, *ugali* with fish, chapatti with *ndengu, pilau* with *kachumbari!* Uuh!Uuh! Good! Since it was morning, he could not ask for any of those dishes. Instead, he mumbled: "Perhaps some tea and bread."

"Alright then," his father said. "Let me see what I can do."

As his father walked out of his room, Agoyi followed him with his eyes until he was completely out of view. Then, a sudden sunken fear ambushed him. Without thinking, he mumbled, "Would father believe me when I tell him the *truth* of what happened? Or would he believe my stepmother's version over mine? What was the *truth?*"

He turned his head, face-up again, but remained still as thoughts of his father continued to torment him. "Father is a just man. As a church minister, he can tell right from wrong. He has to . . . there is no question about that . . . His only flaw is a dash of sternness. I

14

hope that won't overcome his rational senses."

'If his sternness overcomes his goodness, I don't know what I'll do?' Agoyi speculated.

'I have to tell the *truth;* honesty *is* important . . . it develops character and trust. I can't break my father's trust. When trust is broken, relationships suffer,'he mumbled.

"Truth shall set me free, no matter the consequences!" he said. "Yes, truth shall set me free!"

When his father returned moments later, he did not come carrying a tray of food, but a *Standard Newspaper.* The boy's face twisted in a disappointed look.

"The nurse is going to bring you some food in a minute," he announced as he dropped his bottom on the wooden chair like a log. It creaked.

"Thank you!" the boy said, a faint smile appearing at the corners of his mouth.

"How is that thigh of yours?"

"Not bad . . . Just a little pain," Agoyi said wondering how he would tell him what happened or make his confession. "Alright then . . . Baba!" he said timidly.

"Uhh!"

"I have something to tell you about yesterday!"

"I know you do son! I know you do!"

"I'll tell you the *truth,* the whole truth about yesterday!" he said, his voice quivering with fear.

"I know you will son . . . I don't expect anything less from you."

Before Agoyi could make his confession, a nurse walked in carrying a tray of food—two slices of toast, a boiled egg, two sweet bananas, and a cup of steaming tea. She was dressed in her white spotless uniform. As she offered Agoyi his breakfast, an impeccable smile lingered on his face. There was an infectious radiance about her magnified tenfold by the slants of light that fell on her beaming forehead. Her eyes sparkled under the radiant light.

"I have some food here for you," she said, pulling the overbed table in place.

"Thank you!" Agoyi said, scooting slightly in his bed to a throbbing pain in his thigh. She bent forward to prop his back with a pillow.

"Thank you!" Agoyi said again.

"No problem," she said with a smile, rolling the table to reposition it across the bed and slightly above Agoyi's thighs.

"Enjoy!" she said with a smile. "If you needed anything else, let me know," she added, walking out of the room.

The sight of food made him forget his confession to his father as his stomach churned with hunger. He watched steam, from his teacup, spiral upward until it vanished into thin air.

No sooner had Agoyi started eating, than his father opened *The Standard* and started perusing through it, page after page after page, but hardly reading it. Occasionally, he paused whenever he saw an interesting picture or advertisement. Other times, he stole calculated glances at his son, but Agoyi ate in silence, taking small sips of his tea again and again and again . . .

After breakfast, the nurse had already retrieved the dishes, Agoyi seemed subdued, but amiable. His hunger was pacified save for the pain in his thigh that was spreading to his entire side. He gritted his teeth to numb it. Noticing that, Agivondo walked out of the room only to re-emerge with the nurse. The doctor was still tending to patients in Ward 6 and Agoyi had to wait. She gave him some painkillers and walked away.

Once his pain subsided, Agoyi cleared his throat, his

mind cogitated by the previous day's events. His father, who had been 'reading' the newspaper the entire time raised his eyes, folded the newspaper, and dropped it on his lap. He crossed his legs, ogled into his son's eyes, folded his arms around him, and opened his ears as wide as he could to listen.

"My stepmother nearly killed me yesterday!" Agoyi blurted.

His father cocked his heads to face him with keenness.

Agoyi retold his father all the events that led to his assault, from when he returned home, how his stepmother had deliberately not left him any food, his theft, to the assault.

Admittedly, Agoyi said, "I was foolish for stealing. Foolish for thinking: It isn't a moral sin to steal to save a life, *my* life. The Holy book says: 'Thou shalt not steal.' Stealing is a moral sin, I know that too. I was too hungry to think, and the money was too tempting to ignore!"

Even as he made his heartfelt confession, Agoyi thought *his father* would *understand* once he knew the *truth*. After all, he did not buy *bangi* with the money. He bought food. There was nothing wrong with that, or was there?

"My stepmother was guilty of depriving me food!" he told his father.

To that, his father simply said, "Son, what you did was wrong. There is no excuse for stealing. Stealing is stealing and it is plain wrong; it is that simple!Nevertheless, what she did to you is not only morally wrong, but also criminal. Our laws are against such acts, and her fate now rests with the law."

"I understand!"Agoyi noted. A prolonged silence fell between father and son.

When Agivondo spoke again, he was very apologetic, "Son, it was not all your fault."

"What do you mean?" Agoyi said in surprise.

"I am partly to blame!"

"I don't understand!"

"I am the guilty one!"

"I still don't understand."

"I told her last night I was planning to marry a second wife."

"What?"

"Yes! That must have angered her. I am planning to marry a second wife. I wanted to tell her first."

Agoyi was expressionless.

"I have always wanted to have more children," his father continued. "Beyond Laban, she can't have any more children. Wouldn't you like to have another brother or a sister?"

"I thought we were fine the way we were!"

"That is for me to decide," his father said with a hint of irritation in his voice."I think that is why she struck you. . . Your stealing simply gave her reason to strike back at me."

"I see!" Agoyi said with a hint of disappointment in his voice.

"I am sorry for the pain I have caused you!" Agivondo said, dropping his head to the ground, but Agoyi did not add a word.

Both father and son were as far apart as they were present. Agoyi closed his eyes and withdrew into a contemplative silence. His father buried his head in his seat, but his eyes continued to stare outside vacantly through the open window way past the eucalyptus, thriving with activity and life, into the depth of the blue sky. Time did not seem to hurry; it simply settled on their minds like heat at the break of dawn and evaporated like mist at the wake of the rising sun.

Chapter 4

Two weeks after his return from hospital, Agoyi found himself in another fix. That was on a Thursday. Every evening, he and Laban had a regimented schedule: fetch water and chop wood. Whoever chopped wood did not go to the river. Whoever went to the river did not chop the wood. Such was the case on the Thursday Agoyi got in trouble again. He had just returned home from the river when his life changed permanently. Laban was sitting near *kitaraze,* where his mother washed her dishes and toying with his father's *rungu* as though he had nothing to do that evening. Not far from him, was a pile of wood and an axe.

Paying him no attention, Agoyi lowered his pail of water to the ground and dragged it into the stuffy and smoke-filled kitchen. His eyes watered, and he was almost choked by the smoke. He resolved to make a quick in and out exit.

As he walked in, Agoyi remembered to do the right thing: "Good evening mother!" he said.

"Good evening," she said. Her voice was soothing, as though she had already forgotten when she assaulted her stepson. She had pretty much gotten a mere slap on her wrist as the local chief deferred the matter to the family. She begged Agoyi's forgiveness. He had no choice, but simply complied. Though inwardly, he thought, "I'll never forget it as long as I live."

She did not lift her head to look at him. Even if she had, it was impossible to tell. She was busy preparing supper and Agoyi was determined not to stay in the smoke-filled house for only, but a second.

"Has Laban chopped the wood?" she asked.

"I don't know."

"Could you please check?"

"Alright," he said, walking out of the smoke-filled room.

He heaved a sigh of relief as he set foot outside. The air was refreshing and cool.

Immediately, he noticed, as though for the first time, a pile of unchopped wood near *kitaraze.*

"Why haven't you chopped the wood?" Agoyi queried Laban who had been assigned the chore.

"It is *your* job," retorted the snobbish thinly framed and pale faced boy.

"No Laban! That was your chore."

"Mama!" Agoyi called after his step mother. There was no response. "Mama, Laban won't chop the wood."

There was no response.

"*You* chop the wood!" Laban barked.

"No!"

"Mama, make him do it?" Laban yelled.

Again, there was no sound from the kitchen.

Laban who was sitting on the ground, crossed his feet, and adamantly refused to move.

"Fine . . . have it your way," Agoyi said, turning his back away from his half-brother.

"Agoyi!" he heard his stepmother yelling from inside the kitchen. "Could you please chop the wood for me?"

"No!"

"Please!"

"That was Laban's chore . . . Mine was to fetch water!"

"You chop it *right now*, or else . . ." Laban said insolently.

Agoyi stopped in his tracks, but did not turn to look in Laban's direction.

"I told *you* to chop it . . . ha! Didn't I? Didn't I," Laban taunted.

"You two stop that!" Laban's mother said from inside.

"Agoyi . . . You chop it, stupid!" Laban retorted.

Agoyi did not turn back to look at his half-brother. He simply walked off in silence.

"You bastard . . . chop the wood!"

"No brother it's your chore," Agoyi said waving instead and insulted by Laban's comment. He did not dignify the insult with an answer, for he knew he was not a bastard.

He started walking off again. Then, suddenly, something struck him at the back of his head. He stumbled forward, nearly falling. A sharp pain crawled all over his body. He felt a warm trickle spew from the back of his head. He rotated his head in Laban's direction.

Laban was no longer sitting down. In his hand, he still held the giant *rungu* ready to strike him again.

Immediately, Agoyi realized what was happening. "Why did you do that?"

"You are not *my* brother!" Laban yelped. "You, you . . ."

Agoyi pounced on him, struggling to grab the *rungu* away from his hand.

The boys tussled, Laban struggling to hold firm onto his weapon, and Agoyi wanting to take it away from him. Laban punched him in the stomach. Agoyi experienced pain. Then he felt a tingling sensation crop in his hand, and he had no control of it. He rolled his palm in a tightly knotted fist and bit his upper lip until it bled as though he wanted to taste blood. He swiped it dry with his tongue like a chameleon to a fly. When his blood thumping fist struck Laban, he could not stop. He hit him repeatedly, releasing all the anger he harbored within him for years.

"Mama! Mama! Mama! Come quick . . . He is trying to kill me!" Laban yelled.

"You started it!"

"No . . . You did!" They tussled.

"Go back where you came from . . . you! you! . . . You poor excuse for a brother. Go back to your home!"

"I am home!" he retorted.

"No you are not," Laban shot back.

Agoyi punched Laban in the stomach; he screamed.

Laban's mother hearing his screams immediately dashed out of the kitchen wagging a cooking stick in his hand to his son's rescue. She did not care to know what had happened or what had led to the scuffle. Even if she knew, I did not matter, Agoyi was in the wrong, and his son was right. That was all there was to it.

"Make him stop Mama," Laban whined.

"Stop this minute!" she yelled, whacking Agoyi with a cooking stick. Mother and son banded against him.

Not wanting to concede defeat, Agoyi pinned Laban much harder onto the ground as his stepmother rained numerous successive blows upon his body. She did not care where she hit him. The wrath she had held within, from the moment Agoyi had stolen her money, returned. Perhaps, there was more to it. She whacked him again and again and again. Even so, a fight of one between two was no fight at all. Agoyi punched Laban one more time, just as his father arrived home. It was at the point he was on the verge of conceding defeat.

Like his wife, Agivondo did not ask anything. Trembling with anger, he dove into the brawl. His wife stepped out of the way. Without thinking, he yanked Agoyi off Laban, tossing his body to the side.

"Go away from here. You! . . . You! Trouble maker," he barked at Agoyi. He did not bother to find out what happened. He did not care about the *truth*. There was no further *truth* beyond what he had witnessed: Agoyi wanted to *kill* his son.

That was all there was to it. Laban was a saint, and Agoyi the devil.

Taking Laban by the hand, the pair walked into the house, leaving Agoyi outside alone, abandoned.

Agoyi did not move. He watched his father slam the door behind him; it rattled as a giant lump cropped in his throat. Then, he heard the whistling of the wind as it swayed the Jacaranda tree leaves. It was not soothing. He remained silent as his eyes watered and the wind fluttered his tears across his face. He did not move. He just stood there, puzzled. He had no home. He had no place to call home. He was a homeless orphan boy. When the tremor of the door had quieted, he moved his eyes away from the door to the kitchen. His stepmother was standing by the doorway with a giant smile on his face. He said nothing; there was nothing he could say.

That evening, Agivondo decided to evict his son from his home.

Chapter 5

That very night, after his fight with Laban, Agoyi's father plucked him like a weed from Bute village home. There was no discussion regarding the matter. Like any young adult, he had no say. That was the first-time Agoyi saw his father's irrational nature. He was no longer the kind-hearted loving father he had known his entire life. He had made only one mistake, stealing money from his stepmother, for which he had sought forgiveness. He was not the perpetrator in his fight with Laban. Instead of exploring the reasons behind the fight, Agivondo uprooted him from his home and deposited him at his maternal grandparents' home. He believed Agoyi's misbehaviour was a hereditary trait from his mother's family line. He shifted the burden of his care to the old couple. The old man and his wife were now morally obligated to mould him into a perfect young man.

"You are going to stay with your grandparents for a while!"Agivondo had simply declared to his son.

"That is not my home," Agoyi protested. "There are no sugarcanes there."

"That is where you are going to live for now."

"I don't want to go. I like it here!"

"It is only going to be for a little while."

"I don't want to go!"

"It is not in your place to decide. My word is final."

His father packed all his belongings in a suitcase. No, he did not pack everything. He forgot the sugarcane, the bananas, the cassava, the guava tree, the swing in the backyard. They, too, belonged to him. And that was that. He left his childhood home only a few days after he had been discharged from the hospital. That was how Agoyi came to live with his maternal grandparents in Ngoroke Village.

Chapter 6

From the moment Jared Agoyi set foot at his grandparents' home, he knew he was in for trouble. That was at noon. Two hours later, he had been marked by a young man he barely knew. He saw the man intensely watching him through the barbed-wire fence of his grandfather's compound near the acacia tree. The young man was tall, thin, and shabbily dressed in khaki shorts, a dirty-yellow coloured long sleeved T-shirt, and was wearing a red cap. The cap did not quite cover his entire head. It hung slightly above his ears. Dark-brown strands of his knotted hair peered around the edge of the cap. He was narrow-faced, but with an imposing gaze. When their eyes met, his gazes penetrated deep into Agoyi's soul, rendering him defenceless. No simple words could explain that feeling, but he understood what it meant . . . He was branded coincidentally because of his newness to Ngoroke village, and now his new home.

His grandmother, who was probably in her late seventies—at least most people assumed her to be that old—noticed the young man gawking at his grandson like a bird of prey. She quickly emerged from the main house, making her way towards him. The strange boy saw her, but Agoyi was too engrossed in watching him that he did not hear her faint footsteps.

Roughly, she cleared her throat. Startled, Agoyi turned his head in the direction of her sound.

"Agoyi," she said.

"Yes *Guku*!"

"That boy's name is Kahuga," she said, pointing a finger in the direction of the acacia tree where the boy was standing. "He is one of the most imprudent and ill-mannered boys in the entire Ngoroke Village. I don't want you near him as long as you are here."

Befuddled, Agoyi simply stared at his grandmother in silence.

"Do you hear me?"

"Yes . . . Guku!"

"You must avoid him like one avoids a leper. Do you understand? He is a cancer. You must avoid no matter what!"

"Oh!" he gasped as he swerved his head following the direction of his grandmother's finger to where the boy once was, but he had vanished like a whiff of smoke.

"I don't want to see you with him. He is an undesirable riff-raff. Is that clear?" she said affirmatively, a faint smile appearing on her face.

"Yes *Guku*," he said. Feeling vindicated, she walked off towards her kitchen located on the west side of her compound.

Agoyi did not move a muscle as though fossilized. He watched her as she ambled off until she vanished behind her kitchen door. As he stood still and dumbfounded, he tried to understand what had just transpired, but he could not. Confused, his mind raced from the boy whom he had spotted gawking at him to his grandmother's stabbing words of a while ago. He wondered what the young man might have done to be a branded riff-raff. Could his grandmother have misjudged the boy?

He pushed the boy's image off his mind as his past enfolded into the present . . . It was a tarnished past, the very reason his father had forced him to move in with his grandparents. Had his grandmother known *his* truth, *the whole truth, nothing more, but the truth* behind his relocation to Ngoroke, she might have withheld judgement against Kahuga. 'Whatever crime he had committed, I don't know.

Agoyi pushed these thoughts off his mind, conceding that his grandmother was a wise woman and of good moral character. Her judgement of the boy had to be right. Though, inwardly, he thought, 'Whatever he did, perhaps she used poor judgement, just as I did?' Since there can never be smoke without fire, he reversed these views of the young man sooner than he had anticipated . . .

No sooner had Agoyi's grandmother withdrawn into the kitchen than he begun to feel a chocking lump crop-up in his throat. Anger mounted within him like a bad poison. He could not understand why his father had decided to move him to his grandparents' home. Yes, he made a mistake. Who did not? He fought with his half-brother ; wasn't that a norm among siblings? Though, granted, he was branded the black sheep of the family, marked to pay a penalty for the slightest of his transgression. He bore the brunt of his stepmother's hatred. His father had failed to protect him, and he despised him for that, his *abandonment* of him. Soon, tears begun to sting the rims of his eyelids, but he struggled hard to tame them. He turned his eyes away from the direction of the kitchen to the window where he had spotted the young lad moments ago, but he was gone. Slowly, his eyes wandered off away from the window, past the door, past the kitchen to the depth of sky. Giant greying clouds floated in his view and morphed into different shapes: an animal, a bird, a female form. This female visage, lucidly floating the skies, caused his body to shudder as his mind took flight to his mother. Yes, his mother; for she had long departed from the land of the living. He was only a young boy then and he had little to no memory of her . . . virtually no recollection; though, he never stopped imagining what she must have looked like . . .

'Surely, she must have been beautiful, a gentle goddess of the Nile. If she were she still living, would she have protected me?' he wondered. He pushed this thought off his mind saying, 'If she were alive, perhaps father wouldn't have remarried. They would still be together! That is the Logooli way. Logooli men hardly divorce their wives.' Unfortunately, no matter how much he tried to picture his mother, she was as faint on his memory as the floating cloudy form, a priceless figment beyond his reach.

Although death had robbed him a mother, his stepmother had deprived him a father. Still, he blamed Agivondo for most of his follies . . . And this was one of Agoyi's weaknesses, not taking responsibility for his actions. He blamed him for choosing his stepmother over him, ignoring her erratic behaviour and an unending wrath against him—that was the bottom line.

Once again, he reflected on his conundrum: listen to his grandmother's admonition or be like all youths prone to err. 'What to do, what to do!' Poised between two worlds—his old and new home—and as a young boy who honoured boyhood, he was bound to falter, remaining true to his nature of being a conscionable boy, honouring the wishes of his elders, but also yielding to the pressures and dictates of boyhood. Though his thoughts were confounded with the dangers of being branded and the stern warning that followed the branding, the balance of the two was decidedly made in favour of the former. As his mind, once more took flight to the very reason he had left his father's home, he recollected it, not all of it, but most of it to the best of his remembrance . . .

Chapter 7

Ngoroke Village, which had become Agoyi's new home, stood two miles below the apex of Maragoli Hills. It was an exotic place nestled among a grove of scattered bushes and mountainous ridges to the north east of Lake Victoria. Its blue skies, crispy mornings, hot and humid afternoons, and cool nights, made the atmosphere warm and tantalizing to its inhabitants. It was a lonesome place removed from the comforts of modern society, yet a stone throw from the nearby urban centre of Kisumu. From the apex of the hills, one could see the city in a distant horizon. Most of its inhabitants lived in dilapidated round mud-walled and grass thatched farm houses. A few brick-walled homes with zinc-corrugated roof-tops scattered around the village like polka-dots. Most men preferred modern attires, trousers and shirts or T-shirts, while the women clung to their traditional garb of *vitenge* or *kanga* while tending to their children and other domestic chores.

His uncle's hut, which became his residential quarters, was a small brown stucco structure with zinc corrugated roof top, browned under the hash hot weather, and chipped in its corner and located to the south end of his grandfather's compound. His uncle had once told him a jacaranda tree had collapsed on its roof in one thunderous storm, chipping the corner.

To the East of the village, Agoyi saw continuous expanses of ridged stones piled together in giant heaps. These stones forged the infamous *barren* hills of Maragoli. The hills were as dry and barren as the Sahara Desert. It was difficult for Ngoroke natives to believe the hills were once a thick vibrant rainy forest. The forest was destroyed by corrupt politicians and greedy men lured by the love of money, the root cause of all evil. In its place, cluttered low trees and shrubs remained. Whenever it rained, unnatural rivers form, rolling downwards towards the Buhani River like a runaway caboose, sweeping everything in its path: Dead or alive. Man. Woman. Animal. The rain swept everything. Agoyi always wondered where the river emptied its contents. He once asked his grandfather about it. He simply shrugged his shoulders. However, in hind sight, he knew it went all the way to Lake Victoria. The river separated the village from the hills.

To the West of the village, he saw how humongous boulders expanded several miles towards the enigmatic Mung'oma Caves and descended all the way to Maseno. The caves were sacred and believed to be the cradle-base of all Logooli people. The land around the caves was plush and covered with natural exotic vegetation: guava trees, *ovusaangula*—wildberries, ferns, and wild flowers; all forged its vibrant scenery. Right at its base, a spring that never dried continuously hummed silently.

From the stories his grandmother told him, nothing major happened in Ngoroke Village, save for when someone died. Such occurrences were plenty—sometimes it was a child, a mother, a husband, a grandmother, or a grandfather. Only then, would there be action. Nevertheless, nothing could have paralleled what happened only days after his arrival. He heard wailing sounds in the middle of the night. Startled, he sat bolt upright wondering what was going on. Because the night was still dark and dense, he could not go out. He propped his back with a pillow in a reclining manner and listened. Outside, there was tumult, of women shrieking and bemoaning someone . . . A dead neighbour; of male voices, of shuffling feet as people walked hurriedly towards, what he assumed, to be the direction of the ruckus. He did not have a good night.

At daybreak, Agoyi hauled himself from his bed eager to find out what had happened that night. Broken voices of women wailing continued to pierce the morning stillness. He pulled his door open and peeped outside. The air was chilly. He felt a cold breeze gently brush his exposed skin. His body shuddered in its coldness. He pulled his shirt to cover his exposed skin.

As Agoyi stood by the door, he saw a tide of passers-by walking along the narrow footpath by his grandfather's house. A handful of men—four to be precise—stood in a circular formation right at his grandfather's gate. From where he was, their voices floated the air.

"Did you hear what happened," he heard a male voice say.

"Hear what?" came another voice.

"Jumba is dead!"

"Isn't that so?"

"Yes!" the man who had spoken first said. "What you don't know is how he died."

"What happened?" someone asked.

Hearing that, Agoyi leaned on the door ledge to listen. His ears were now attuned to the early morning gossip.

"From what I heard, he was murdered!"

"Murdered! Murdered?" the men exclaimed.

"Yes! . . . He was murdered?"

"By whom?" the men queried, almost in unison.

"By his cousin Asah!"

"Really? That is unbelievable."

"It came from his own mouth."

"You don't say!"

"This is what they said: 'The two men had been drinking together at Asah's house for hours. By midnight, Jumba bade Asah bid good-bye. Only, when he walked out of his cousin's house, and he had shut his door,

Jumba didn't quite go home. He marched to his cousin's vegetable garden where he started harvesting his *sukuma*. Hearing the ruckus outside, Asah walked out of the house and, in a drunken stupor, mistook him for a thief. He pierced his heart with a knife. Jumba died of his wound."

"That is not true!" someone said.

"That is not true! To kill someone because of *sukuma* cannot be true!" another man added, shaking his head despondently.

"That is just half of the story," the man continued.

"Is there more?"

"Oh . . . Oh, you haven't heard all of it!"

"Do tell!"

"What he did was even more sinister than his cousin's killing. Asah walked back into his house, took a hoe and shovel and dug the man's grave right in his compound."

"You don't say!"

"Yes indeed! He dug a grave in the night, buried the man and after he had covered his grave, he adorned it with the *sukuma* the man had harvested. He then went to his father's home, where he confessed his crime."

"The things that happen these days are beyond my understanding," someone said.

"It was his father who ratted him out to the police! Can you believe that? His own father turned him to the police."

"Wololo! Our world has turned upside down: A brother killing his brother. A father not saving his son. A mother abandoning her children. We are doomed to rot in hell!"

Like the men at the gate, Agoyi could not believe his ears. Such things never happened in Bute Village. He walked back to his room and there he sat for a long time. What a story! His father will never believe it . . .

When Agoyi finally emerged from the house an hour later, he walked to his grandfather's, but he had already gone to Jumba's home to see what happened. His grandmother had just finished preparing breakfast: tea and cassavas.

"Have some tea son!" she commanded, offering her a cup and plate of cassavas.

"Thanks *Guku!*" Agoyi took the cup and started seeping it silently.

Later, Agoyi asked his grandmother's permission to visit Jumba's home. He, too, wanted to bear witness to the fantastic story. She granted him his wish. That was the most action Agoyi witnessed in Ngoroke village. That was before he got entangled in Kahuga's web of mischief . . .

The only other kind of *entertainment* in Ngoroke came at dawn, when the voice of Irene, a village recluse woman, pierced the morning daybreak in prayer, to the chagrin of many contented by rooster's early crowing. She was a newly converted Christian and believed everyone in Ngoroke deserved to know God. Not just *knowing* God, but they, too, had to be converted to the new faith. That is why at the dawning of each day, she yelped and prayed for all the villagers. Save their souls. Her prayer, more often than not,was followed by an annoying heavy drumming and unsynchronized singing:

Kindu cha ndanyoola ne ling'ana	*What I have received is the Word*
Luuya	*Luuya*
Kindu cha ndanyoola ne ling'ana	*What I have received is the Word*
Luuya	*Luuya*
Vaandu va voolange ndaalaluka	*People might say I am mad*
Luuya	*Luuya*
Vaandu va voolange ndaalaluka	*People might say I am mad*
Luuya	*Luuya*

Her shrill voice was more annoying than soothing. She howled and squealed until the sun peeked above the misty hills of Maragoli. Only then, when she had begun to feel the golden warmth from the sun, see the dancing breeze waving with streaks of light above the hills, only then, she abandoned her howling, withdrawing back into her house as though nothing had happened.

Most people in the village did not mind her. She was the time clock that summoned their dawn hour. Like most people, Agoyi loathed that hour of dawn, for Irene was such a nuisance. She even reminded him of the annoying crows he had seen while at the hospital nursing his injury. Had she been Bute Village, he might have organized a raid against her. Teach her a lesson or two. Eventually, he concluded that given the many mornings Irene prostrated in prayer, when she died, she would go straight to heaven. Whatever that was, for he hardly believed in it. There was no other place for her, but heaven. Hell would be too harsh of a punishment for her.

This was Agoyi's new environment, and he did not like it. Then, he thought about his Bute village: so quiet and peaceful! He missed it a hell lot more than he admitted to himself. He even wished he could go back. Most of all, he yearned to swing on his swing. He wanted to get sugarcane from his *shamba*. He wanted to eat fresh cassavas. He wanted everything from Bute, but conceded that things were useless childish dreams. Running away was as useless as the dream itself. Surely, he was paying a heavy price for his mistake—stealing a measly twenty shilling note.

At Ngoroke, there were no children in his grandparents' home. There was no one to play with, unless if he made new friends. Nevertheless, the only person whom he had seen watching him, he had been warned to avoid. What was he to do then?

Chapter 8

Three days after his arrival in Ngoroke Village, Agoyi came face to face with his nemesis, Kahuga.

That morning, Agoyi woke-up to his grandfather's tapping sound on his door.

"Agoyi! Are you up?"

There was no answer.

"Agoyi! Are you awake?" the Oldman said again.

Still, there was no answer.

Assuming the young man to be sound asleep, he tapped the door a little harder.

"Agoyi, Agoyi, Agoyi!" he tapped on the door again and again and again and his tapping grew louder and louder.

Startled from his sleep and ruffled in his covers, Agoyi nearly fell as he jumped out of bed.

"Agoyi!" the Oldman said again.

"Yes *Guga*," Agoyi said as he hurriedly rushed out of his bedroom hopping on one foot while trying to put on his pants.

"Agoyi!"

"Yes *Guga*," a scruffy Agoyi said, turning the latch on his door. He pulled it open. His grandfather was standing at the door with his right foot on the first step.

"Your grandmother tells me she is out of sugar. Could you go to the shop and buy her some?"

"Yes *Guga!*" he said, wiping sleep matter out of his eyes. "But I don't know where it is."

"It is very simple," the Oldman said handing him a hundred shilling note. "Walk through that gate, turn left and then right at the junction. Go up the hill. The shop is less than a quarter of a mile from the junction. It is on the left. You will see it."

"No problem *Guga*," Agoyi said taking the money. He did not bother to wash his face.

"Hurry-up, will you?"

"Yes *Guga*," he said, sprinting towards the gate.

This was his first outing since his arrival in Ngoroke. The morning was like no other, and the air was cool and soothing. Way yonder to the eastern hemisphere, the sun struggled to ascent above the misty glow of Maragoli Hills. The trail to the shop was a grassy winding narrow footpath covered with dew. Agoyi felt its cool chillness right to the core of his bones, as his bare feet came in contact with it. That did not matter very much to him. Instead, he kept on trying to dodge patches of wet grass as he looked for dry spots. As he hobbled along, playing hopscotch with dew covered and dry spots in his path, he ran into none-other-than Kahuga right at the junction. He remembered him as the same boy he had seen gawking at him at his grandfather's home.

Kahuga was a shabby looking fellow. Crusted sleep matter was still in his eyes. His hair was not only uncombed, but it looked as though someone had deliberately rubbed his hands through it, leaving strands of knotted locks on his head. His maroon shirt was not only wrinkled, but also torn around his elbows, exposing his dry ashen skin. He looked like a vagrant. He was still wearing his red cap.

"Where do you think you are going?" the boy growled.

Startled, Agoyi stopped, his eyes gaping wide into those of the scraggly looking fellow. By comparison, Agoyi was probably slightly taller than him—about five-eight. Being new to the village, Agoyi was simply flabbergasted by the question.

"Are you deaf?" the boy barked. "Agoyi basically looked at him. I said, where do you think you are going?"

Feeling threatened, Agoyi queried, "Do I know you?"

"You can't answer a question with a question— dumb goat!" Agoyi did not answer. He stared at him dumbfounded. "I said, where do you think you are going?" the boy roared with clenched teeth.

"It is none of your business!"

"You are a gutsy fella aren't you," the boy said circling him like a rooster that had just cornered a hen. Agoyi shrug his shoulders.

"Do you know who I am?" the boy said more menacingly than before and moving up close into his face.

"Not really and I don't care," Agoyi said. An inner voice entreating him, '*run, run, run,*' but he could not run away from a conflict. Running was cowardly and he was no coward.

"Those who know me call me Kahuga the Beast," he said boisterously. "Since you don't know me, I can either be your worst nightmare, or your best friend," he said poking him in his shoulder.

"Don't do that!" Agoyi said retaliating with a push.

"Or else what?" he raved, shoving Agoyi.

"Don't do that!" Agoyi said, irritated. "I warn you!" In a split second, rampant thoughts crept on his mind, 'Was *Guku* right about Kahuga? What if he was the worst being in Ngoroke?'Then his grandmother's words flashed his mind, *"Avoid him like one avoids a leper. Avoid him . . . avoid him . . . avoid him."* These words kept on ringing on his mind like a broken record. 'Perhaps the old lady was right!'

"I make it my problem to make my acquaintance with any riff-raff who comes into this village," Kahuga said, interrupting his thoughts.

"Excuse me . . . Kahuga, but I have to go," Agoyi said walking around him and avoiding the conflict altogether. Kahuga forced his scrawny body in front of Agoyi, blocking his way.

"I wouldn't do that if I were you?"

"And why not?"

"Because I am still talking to you!"

"Listen man," Agoyi said goaded by Kahuga's obstruction. "*Guga* sent me on an errand. I plan to complete it," he said forcefully shoving Kahuga out of his way. Kahuga's feet gave way from under him as he tumbled down hard on a dew covered footpath. Feigning to be hurt, he sprawled his body on the wet ground.

Agoyi did not stand around to see whether he was hurt or not. He straddled out of his way heading west towards the shop. As he walked up-hill, he turned two or three times to see if the boy was still on the ground. And he was still sprawled on the ground.

"Serves him right!" he mumbled, though he could not understand why Kahuga was still laying down. He had not meant to push him too hard, but that did not matter anymore. "He asked for it!" he mumbled. Then he remembered the Oldman's last words: *"Hurry-up, will you?"* He took several steps again, stopped, and turned in the direction of the boy. He was still on the ground. If he had harmed him, he might be in a heap of trouble. Not only that, he will have some explaining to make when he came face-to-face with the Oldman or Kahuga's folks. 'What if he twisted his leg?' he speculated.

When he reached the shop, he purchased a packet of sugar and hurriedly raced downhill towards the injured boy. Kahuga was no longer where he had left him; instead, he had balled-up his body as though writhing in agony. A cold shiver ran down his spine again. There was no justification for fighting, even though he could not call what transpired a fight. He merely defended himself.

As he drew closer to Kahuga, the boy was sobbing profusely as though nursing a broken ankle. He was a pitiful sight. Filled with remorse and trepidation, Agoyi raced harder towards him, under the brilliant morning sun, his heart pounding copiously. He could barely see ahead because of the sun's blind rays. That did not stop him, he ran, nonetheless. The fear of being perceived as a troublemaker and the punishment that followed deeply cogitated his mind. No sooner had he got to the boy, than he put his packet of sugar on the ground by the injured boy's side. Bending over him to see if he was alright, before he even asked him, 'Are you alright?' Kahuga startled him. Wham! Bang! He smashed him in the crotch with his right foot and seizing his sugar. A shockwave of pain crawled all over his body. Agoyi grabbed his loins as he straddled backwards and unable to walk. Duped, he felt tears sting the rims of his eyes.

A victorious Kahuga rose-up with a cheerful expression, dusted, and walked-up to Agoyi. Threateningly, he said: "If you cross me again, you'll be sorry you did. Do you understand?" His cheerful expression faded as fast as it had appeared on his face.

Agoyi lifted his eyes, giving him a mean stare.

"Don't ever cross me. Do you understand?"

Agoyi nodded.

"I want you to know I am the untouchable haughty fox of Ngoroke . . . You don't mess with me! Am I making myself clear?"Defeated, Agoyi nodded once again.

"Now, you'll do exactly as I say. Do you understand?" a braggadocios Kahuga said. Agoyi nodded again.

"If not, you won't know what hit you," Kahuga added.

"What do you want?" Agoyi said angrily.

"This evening . . ."

"What?" Agoyi queried, not even giving Kahuga a chance to complete his thought.

"I want to tell you something!"

"Why can't you say it now?"

"I said this evening . . . don't you have ears?"

"I can't!"

"That is your problem . . . Be ready when I come for you!"

"How will I know you are there?"

"The same way I saw you looking at me yesterday!"

"I see!"

"You didn't think I noticed?"

"No!"

"Be there and ready when I come or else you will be sorry. Am I making myself clear?"

"Crystal clear!"

"It is settled then . . . this evening!"

"May I have *my* sugar back?"

"Not so fast!"

"Now what?"

Kahuga hesitated for a moment. "Come here," he said.

Without a word, Agoyi obeyed. Kahuga whispered something in his left ear.

"Okay!" Agoyi said reluctantly.

"Then it is settled . . . Here take your sugar," Kahuga said handing him the packet with a grin. As Agoyi stretched his hand and reached for it, Kahuga retrieved it teasing him. Agoyi's face muscles tightened with displeasure.

"Am sorry, I was just kidding," Kahuga said, handing Agoyi his sugar. He took it without a word and started walking away. He did not look back even if he felt Kahuga's eyes piercing his back. He walked swiftly until he got home.   His grandmother had already finished making their morning tea.

That morning, Agoyi committed his first act of disobedience against his grandmother. He had allowed himself to be blackmailed on his initial outing out of his grandfather's compound, and that was just the beginning of his troubles . . .

Chapter 9

Darkness was approaching when Agoyi finished milking the cows. He took it to his grandmother and walked into his hut. Feeling worn and low-spirited, he dropped his body in the chair like a log. There he sat sullenly awaiting supper. In his depressed state, he thought about all the bad things that had happened in his life, forcing him from home indefinitely. 'How foolish I was,' he thought. 'And that fight, that fight with Laban, what an unexpected fiasco . . . definitely unexpected. It made my strained relationship with my folks worse.' Then his thoughts floundered to Kahuga and the fight, though it was not much of a fight. Call it entrapment. He cursed himself for yielding to his unwarranted blackmail. 'What was the justice in the physical threats he received from Kahuga? He cursed his newness to Ngoroke. Had he been in his Bute Village, he could have defended himself. Ngoroke was not his turf. He was reeled back to his consciousness when, suddenly, he heard a voice from outside:

"Psst! Psst! Psst!" There was silence. He listened now more keenly. Perhaps, his ears were playing a cruel trick on him.

"Psst! Psst! Psst! Agoyi," he heard the sound again. The sounded was much louder than it had the first time.

Begrudgingly, he dragged his body from the chair and shuffled his feet lazily towards the window. His head slowly shot-up behind the dusty tainted and cracked window of his uncle's house. He did not see anything or anyone. He ducked his head down, wondering if there was a ghostly visitation beyond the fence of his grandfather's homestead. Such visitations were not uncommon. He could not fathom having an encounter with a spectre . . . That would be catastrophic.

"Psst! Agoyi," came the voice again. "It's me, Kahuga." Agoyi slowly, but surely pushed his head up; and leaning on the cold dusty glass, he ogled the area behind his uncle's ramshackle house again. He could not see anyone or anything yet!

"Where are you?" he forced himself to say with restless confidence, knowing fully that if anyone were to see him speaking to no one, in particular, he would declare him mad. Nevertheless, he was not mad.

"Here!" the voice said again. Agoyi's eyes roamed aimlessly, from tree to tree, branch to branch, way beyond the fence.

"Here!" the voice said again. Agoyi's eyes followed the sound of the voice. Then, from behind an acacia tree, a smiling head popped-up. And there, he saw him, Kahuga Aduda, a boorish young man, standing behind the tree. His unkempt hair was tucked underneath a red cap. He was such a character. His clothes were patches of different coloured fabric: blue, green, yellow, orange and brown. It was nearly impossible to guess the original colour of his attire.

Kahuga winked a suggestive wink. Agoyi reciprocated with a nod.

Agoyi moved away from the window, and instead of sitting down, he raced to his bedroom. It was dark in there that he could barely see. He stabbed one of his toes on his bed post, squealing in pain. No joy here! He bent forward, puckered his lips in a round firm "O" and forced cool air on the toe. The injured toe was seething with so much hurt that he felt no satisfaction from his action. He quickly abandoned this whole silly effort of easing the pain by blowing air on it.

Stooping forward, he leaned his face close to the guardrail of his bed and gradually thrust his right hand underneath it. He felt something soft and furry. Quickly, he retrieved his hand . . . Not what he expected. 'Couldn't be a rat or could it?' he mumbled to himself. His body shook in fright at the thought of having touched a disease infested rodent. He wanted to rush outside, grab a *rungu*, dash back, and bludgeon the little furry creature to death, but that was foolish. That action would draw the Oldman's attention to the ruckus in his hut. He could not do that. The Oldman had to be kept at bay, just for the evening.

"Psst! Psst!" he heard the voice again.

He dashed back to the window. "In a minute!" he whispered. Kahuga was still standing snobbishly behind the acacia tree. He had a cheerful expression, but it faded as Agoyi ran back to his bedroom. He pushed his hand again underneath the bed and pulled something out. He paused for just a second, looked at it, and then shoved it under his shirt. He grabbed his brown feather-light jacket and headed for the door. When he got to the centre of the living room, he stopped to listen. Afraid to be seen, he tiptoed toward the door.

Gently, he pushed his head through the door. The air outside was pitilessly raw and cold. Its chilliness penetrated deeply on his exposed skin. He could not dare step outside, at least, not yet. His eyes rotated in his sockets much like a thief's would, afraid of being caught. He moved them from right to left and, then again, left to right! He rolled them sideways, to his grandmother's kitchen; a thick curl of smoke spiralled upwards and frizzled into empty space. He could only imagine what she was cooking in there: a gigantic pot of beef stew bubbling over her makeshift Japanese stove. The sweet smells of freshly sautéed onions, roasted garlic, and Simba Mbili curry powder filled the air. He licked his chops as he imagined how he would later satiate his hunger on her savoury dish.

To his right, the Oldman's front door, which faced east and overlooked the hills, was ajar. He sighed despairingly, wondering whether the Oldman was sitting in his favourite cheap red leather chair in the living room facing the entrance. Old adage—it is bad luck to have one's back to the entrance—precluded him from doing so. His image, of a tall heavy-set man with shoulders as broad as a bull, forced a chill down Agoyi's spine. He was the kind of man who could easily crush him like a bug with his bare feet. For, if he were sitting in his living room, he would definitely see him, and he did not want that to happen. He was certain that if he caught a glimpse of him, he would yell at him: "Wewe kijana, kuja hapa—Young man, come here!" Yes, he knew and understood what he would say; after all, he had committed to memory his entire routine. Just the thought of the Oldman stopping him caused his heart to pound rapidly. He could not let that happen. No. No matter what, he had to evade him or risk being branded by Kahuga.

Without thinking, he forced his head back inside the house. The air was musty and humid. All he needed was a strategy. That is it, a good solid plan to leave the house unnoticed.

Pressing his back on the wall, he imagined several ways to escape unnoticed: He could get a saw, cut through the steel bars of his uncle's window. That way, he could escape the Oldman's compound anytime he wished. He pondered this option just for a moment and disbanded it almost immediately. It was stupid! He could not do it. The sound of sawing metal would only alert the Oldman of his intent. As he contemplated his next move, he remembered his grandmother's stern warning: *"As long*

*as you are living under my roof, you must avoid him like
one avoids a leper!"* His body shuddered at the thought
of disobeying her. Then, a bright idea struck him. 'Yes,
I'll march right into the Oldman's house, strike a cheap
conversation with him, and then vanish through the back
door.' Before his idea crystallized in his mind, he heard
Kahuga's shrill, but urgent voice:

"Psst! Psst! Make it quick man!"

Afraid of the threat of physical harm, Agoyi grumpily
grumbled, "I've got to get out of here!"

Regaining some courage, he pried his body off the wall,
pushed his head through the door and made a quick
sweep of the entire compound once more to the pounding
of his heart. There was no one in close vicinity. With
the course clear, he thrust his right foot outside in slow
motion, lugging his left foot forward. Like lightning, he
swerved to the left, sprinting to the back of the hut. When
he was safe, concealed behind the house, he stopped
abruptly, took a deep breath, and turned back to be sure
no one had seen him. No one had. He let out a deep
sigh of relief as he turned, yet again, heading towards the
fence. No sooner had he turned than the object he had
hidden under his shirt slipped out, landing on his injured
toe.

"Rats!" he exclaimed in pain. "That was too unexpected,"
he said hopping up and down like a rabbit. When pain
in his toe subsided, he crawled through the fence and
out of the homestead to where Kahuga was standing. He
reprimanded him for his snobbish behaviour of pestering
him about coming out: "Don't ever do that again."

Once the boys were beyond earshot, they walked
quietly southbound towards the road. At the junction,
the road forked out: one heading east and the other west.
They turned left, strolling eastward towards the primary
school. Kahuga was now jovial, but Agoyi remained

indifferent.

"Do you have it?" Kahuga said almost immediately.

"Have what?"

"You know what I mean!"

"What if I don't?"

"As I said before," Kahuga said, biting his lips. "You don't want me to jot your name in my bad book. Do you?"

"What difference does it make?"

"So, do you have it? Kahuga queried, ignoring Agoyi's remark.

"Of course . . . I always keep my word," Agoyi said boisterously.

"I knew it! I knew it. For a moment, I thought you had been struck by a conscience," Kahuga said with a mischievous giggle.

"Yeah right!" he said jokingly. Of course it was the physical threat of being beaten that forced his submission to *blackmail*.

"You must be kidding! . . . I don't remember the last time that happened to me."

"If you have it, where is it?"

"What is your hurry?"

"Something tells me you are pulling my leg."

"And which leg of yours might I be pulling," Agoyi said with a giggle. "The third leg?"

"Spare me the ridicule!"

"All right then! . . . If you must see it," he paused, looked at Kahuga, and pushed his right hand in his jacket as though he was about to pull *it* out, but, on second thought, he changed his mind.

"You don't have *it*! And that is the plain truth."

"You son of a goat . . . If I have *it*, what will you give me?"

"I'll tell you as soon as we get to Lidaala."

"It better be something good!"

"Of course yes! What do you take me for?"

"A big joker!"

"Am serious . . . If am not wrong, you will thank me for the rest of your life."

"Are you sure about that?"

"Dead sure!"

"Alright then." Convinced of his friend's intentions, Agoyi pulled a bottle from inside his jacket. It was filled to the brim with a milky substance. "Here!" he commanded, pushing the bottle towards Kahuga. "Take it before I change my mind."

Kahuga grinned. "Wow, you are something aren't you? How did you do it?"

"You don't want to know. And so you know; I am not proud of my actions. There is something askew about stealing from the hand that feeds you!"

The boys walked together towards Lidaala, a gigantic stone, which was as flat as a pancake and expanded over a radius of a mile. The pathway towards the stone snaked downwards through a shady meandering stony footpath. They had to fight shrubbery along the way and be careful enough not to bang their toes on the stones. They stooped constantly to avoid scratching their heads on tree branches. Dead flies and other insects trapped in webs hung on tree limbs. The boys continued their stroll like two lovers oblivious to their surrounding, wrapped-up in their own world.

Then they heard a rustle in the bush and a twig snapping. Agoyi pushed Kahuga forward, his heart beginning to pound. They stopped to listen. Afraid of snakes, no—paranoid of snakes, Agoyi wondered if the noise they had heard was the slithering sound of a black mamba, the deadliest snake in Ngoroke village. The sound died down as the boys came to a screeching halt. Way below them, they caught a glimpse of a monkey hopping from stone to stone. A sparrow leaped and chirped. Amid a gaping crack at a nearby stone, a groundhog's head shot up and vanished as rapidly as it emerged. The boys remained still as though their feet had been weighted with lead; only their minds remained active, thwarted with thoughts of their impending danger. They were too afraid to continue with their downward trek.

Still stupefied, they heard the howling of a monkey a few yards below them. Agoyi's eyes raced downward in the direction of the racket. A monkey barely standing firmly on a banana plant struggled to yank a green fruit from its tree, but the fruit was stubborn and unyielding. Then, with a strong show of force, she pulled one measly banana off the tree and shoved it in her mouth, making an attempt to peel it. Mechanically, and with the use of her teeth, she ripped open the outer layer of the fruit, which she tossed to the ground. She shoved the peeled banana in her mouth and scuttled off.

Kahuga turned his eyes away from the monkey to Agoyi who was as frightened as a rat in a trap. He looked so funny that Kahuga balled-up, laughing delightfully to his friend's chagrin. Above them, a hawk glided gracefully above the village in the clear blue sky, searching to usurp an unsuspecting chick.

"Let us go," Agoyi finally mumbled. The boys continued their trek downhill until they arrived at Lidaala.

No sooner had they arrived than Agoyi became frightened by the sheer massiveness of the rock. The landscape of his former Bute Village was flat. No hills. No giant stones. No massive rocks. Lidaala was a giant rock, wide, round, and steep. He had never seen a rock

as massive as the one before him. It frightened him by
its utter immensity. And the mere thought of hiking it,
or crawling all the way to its apex, tightly knotted the
muscles of his stomach. He had not climbed anything
like it before, though he had had plenty of practice on
guava trees. Gathering courage, the boys began their
ascension, crawling up the slippery stone-like ants on
an anthill; their bare sweaty feet slipping every so often
with each climb. They moved robotically, huffing and
puffing with every step they took. Kahuga's foot slipped
as he made his way upward. He squealed out of fear.
He quickly grabbed firmly on the stone. Agoyi held his
breath, scared to his wits' end lest the inevitable happen.
A sudden slip from the rock, sending his friend's body
tumbling down to the caves which separate the village
from the hills, would have been tragic. He imagined how
his body would be reduced to a pile of scrambled mash
over the hard rocks. Vultures would have a feast on his
remains. He pushed these thoughts off his mind as he
steadied himself, continuing with the climb. Sparrows
and crows glided the skies, and he envied them.

Agoyi let out a despairing sigh! Regaining composure,
Kahuga continued with his climb. One foot at a time, he
crept way up to the stone. Tiny beads of sweat formed on
his upper lip, but he hardly paid attention. His mind was
set on the rock, nothing more or nothing less. One step.
Two steps. On the third, he slipped again.

"Agoyi," he said fretfully. "You may have to help
me!"That was strange because Agoyi thought Kahuga
would not have any difficult climbing the rock, but he
did. He was only full of hot air and less action. He later,
he learned Kahuga had never climbed that rock before.

Agoyi turned his head downwards to look at Kahuga,
but instead his eyes glossed over beyond him, becoming

fixated on the slope below them. Once more, a bad thought crept over his mind, 'What would happen to Kahuga were he to slip downwards?' Could he be charged with his death were that to happen? He tried to push these thoughts off his mind, but they remained a forceful enigma on his psyche. He moved his eyes from the base of the rock back to his friend, but he was as frightened as a rat at the sight of a cat.

"Okay . . . Tell you what!" he said. "When I get on top of the rock, I will throw you my belt. Grab onto it tightly and use your other arm and legs to push up!"

"That sounds dumb!"

"You have a better idea?"

Kahuga shook his head. "What if I slip and fall?"

"Well, you know the answer to that one . . . The very reason you cannot afford to lose focus!"

"All right then . . . I will try it!" he said unconvincingly.

Agoyi climbed meticulously, while Kahuga hung on the peripheral with a nervous watch.

Once at the top, Agoyi unhooked his leather belt, which he threw down to Kahuga.

"Grab on it tightly!" Agoyi instructed.

"Okay!" Kahuga yelled, trying to grab it, but missed. His left foot slipped from under him, and he slid downwards. Agoyi gasped.

"No problem . . . Let us try again!" Agoyi yelled.

"Careful man! . . . Hold tight. You don't want to be food for the vultures, do you?" Agoyi queried.

"Not really!" Kahuga said as he steadied himself, lunged forward and remained still.

Agoyi lowered the belt to him again. He grabbed onto it tightly with his right hand, not wanting to let go of his firm grip on the rock. He heaved a sigh of relief as his fingers latched onto the belt, but he did not pull.

"Okay, on the count of three, I will pull, and you should try to lunge forward."

"Okay."

"One. Two. Three!" Agoyi pulled the belt, and Kahuga leapt forward like a cat. He did not make it to the top.

"Again!" Agoyi said for a second time. As he was about to find a safe landing, the unexpected happened. The bottle his friend had given him earlier slipped from under his shirt, tumbling down in a rapid descent. Kahuga moved his eyes from the belt, which was now barely securing his safety, to the bottle. He followed it with his eyes as it hopped downwards like a rabbit. All he could hear was: "Doof! Doof! Doof!" and with a loud bang, "twaaaaa" it burst open, breaking into small pieces and its contents splashing all over the rock. "That could have been me," Kahuga said sadly. And, at that point, nerves made his stomach tighten like banded steel.

"What a splatter!" Agoyi said. His big round eyes gleamed furtively from the remnants of the bottle to his friend. Beaming with a deceptive hope, he added, "I am glad it wasn't me!"

"That is what I get for *stealing* milk from an old man who has done nothing to me. The gods must be watching over him," Kahuga added. Though the truth was Kahuga had forced Agoyi to steal the milk from the Oldman. He had threatened him with physical harm if he did not make good of his request.

Kahuga eyeballed Agoyi, who understood the meaning of his stare. Quietly, Agoyi lowered his belt again. Kahuga grabbed it. With one pull and a powerful push, Kahuga found his safe landing on the rock. Although beads of sweat had begun to form on his brow, he did not care. All that mattered was his safety, and he was safe. Elated he had made the climb and lived to tell about it; he plopped his bottom on the hard cold bedrock crisscrossing his legs. Admiringly, his eyes ogled the steep embankment that descended all the way to the Buhani River. Red soil around jam-packed stones forged its beautiful natural landscape. The boys could now hear the river's soft murmur as they sat on the rock. They could also hear sounds of spider monkeys yelping in the shrubbery, while groundhogs played hide and seek games with each other.

The boys leaned backward, gently lowering their backs onto the hard cold rock. Up above its hard smooth surface, they felt safe; an utmost sense of serenity enveloped them, bringing solace to their mind, body, and soul. Their eyes stared rigidly into the deep-blue sky. Hawks glided with ease, soaring up high and taking sudden tumbling dives downwards. Their bodies sliced through the clouds, as though they were about to plunge into the crevice of earth, but did not. The boys watched the spectacle in mute silence for a very long time . . .

Chapter 10

By seven, the sun was almost down, but the boys still lay on the rock in mute silence. Sparrows, hawks, pigeons flew in their view, but they remained quiet in their watching. They gazed into the open space, as far and wide as the eye could see, but hardly seeing. Agoyi's mind had recoiled back onto his past, to the very reason his father had uprooted him from home: stealing and fighting with Laban. Yes, he was an enigma boy in motion, buoyed by his past. An inner voice within reminded him of the perils of stealing and fighting. 'Stealing brings death. Stealing is a moral sin. There is no forgiveness for such act.' He bit his lower lip. He blamed his father for his mistake. 'Fighting was just as bad, especially if the world bands against you,' he speculated.

"Agoyi," Kahuga said after a prolonged silence.

Agoyi did not respond.

"Agoyi!" Kahuga said again.

Agoyi turned towards Kahuga, but remained soundless.

"I am a man of few words so I'll get right to the point."

"What is it?"

"I have a proposition for you!"

"Proposition . . . what do you mean a *proposition*?" Agoyi said mimicking him as though he did not understand the word.

Kahuga nodded. "I have a proposition for you."

"Why do you think I might be interested in your . . . What did you call it?"

"*Proposition!*"

"Yes, *proposition!* Why do you think I might be interested?"

"It is just a hunch!"

"I am not interested!"

"You are here aren't you?"

"Because you made me."

"You could have refused . . . but you are here."

"You threatened me, don't you remember?"

"You could have refused. I didn't put a knife to your throat. . . but you are here, which tells me that you are willing to . . ."

"Willing to do what?" Agoyi said irritated.

"To do as I tell you!"

"I think you are mistaken."

"Let us not get worked-up about this."

"Worked-up! Worked-up?"

"Calm down . . . all I am saying is: I have a *proposition* for you."

"Am not interested."

"Just listen. If you don't like it, you don't have to do it . . . I know you might find it interesting."

Agoyi did not say a word. He shifted his weight on the cold solid rock, his eyes gaping into open space again. He saw nothing. Instead, he felt Kahuga's eyes piercing his sides. A meaningful moment of silence elapsed between them. Agoyi's mind took flight to his past again. He recalled the last time *a friend* had lured him into a neighbour's home to steal mangoes. The mangoes were huge, ripe, and enticing. He knew it was wrong, but he did it; he could not resist the temptation. That was not the worst part. When they got caught, he got entangled in a web of deceit—which was worse than the very act of stealing. He feigned innocence, instead of conceding his guilt, of being a willing accomplice, just as he was in stealing milk from the Oldman. His worst crime was: he had lied to his father about it, a cultural taboo. The punishment he received for that *minor* infraction exceeded the actual crime—four strokes on his posterior with a leather belt for each mango he had stolen—twelve canes in total. His father ordered him not to make a sound as the belt crushed on his posterior. He bit his lower lip as successive strokes cut through his tender flesh. He vowed never to fall in a similar trap again. But now he was facing a similar bait and did not know how to escape it.

Agoyi turned his head again to face Kahuga. Their eyes met, but there was virtually no expression in his eyes, just a hard deep penetrating gaze.

"I am sorry Kahuga, but I am not interested!" he mumbled.

"I am doing you a favour . . . don't you see?"

"I am not interested in your favour!"

"You don't mean that."

"Oh, but I do!"

"You don't want to meet some of the guys in Ngoroke Village?"

"Not really?"

"Why not?"

"Am not interested, can't you get that through your thick skull!"

There was no change in Agoyi's reaction; his face remained expressionless.

"I have this small group . . ." Kahuga said again, sizing Agoyi. Agoyi was as immobile as the boulder upon which they were laying. "Yes, we call it Haughty Boys!"

Agoyi's demeanour was unchanged. "You might find these guys interesting. They will keep you busy and out of trouble, being new and all that here . . . or when you are lonely and miss home, they'll be there for you."

Agoyi clamped his jaws so tight the veins in his neck felt as though they would burst. Truly, he missed his home. He missed his friends. He missed his father. Not his half-brother. Definitely, not his stepmother. He was not ready to venture into a group. He had his grandmother. He had his grandfather. Wasn't that enough? He was not ready to join any group. Not even Haughty Boys of Ngoroke.

"No one is going to force you into joining," Kahuga pressed. "Just take it as an experiment . . . some kind of trial. Mind you, I can't guarantee the others'acceptance of you. If they find you appealing, you can join the group. If you like the group, you may join. You are free to leave it anytime you want!"This turned out to be a lie.

Out of curiosity, Agoyi queried, "What kind of expectations do you have of your members?"

"You have to join first to know! That is the group policy. No, I'll give you a secret: Each new inductee has to prove his worthiness by performing one act."

Agoyi did not say anything. A brief silence followed.

"This doesn't involve doing anything illegal . . . does it?"

"Hahaha!" Kahuga burst into a cynical laughter.

"Just want to know!"

"Maybe it is and maybe it is not! You have to join first. Otherwise, we do not reveal group secrets to none members."

"What kind of secrets do you have?"

"I can't tell you that. I can't betray my group."

Agoyi moved his head away from Kahuga staring rigidly up into the depth of sky. Massive grey clouds glided with ease. A sparrow flew above, but he was undisturbed by it. He remained profoundly still. Distantly, he could hear the sound of the whistling wind as it swayed tree branches near the base of the rock, ushering onto his mind the sullen voice of his grandmother as she sternly warned him against Kahuga: *"He is one of the most imprudent and ill-natured boys in the whole of Ngoroke Village . . . avoid him like one avoids anyone afflicted with leprosy! He is a cancer you should evade at all cost."* Agoyi wondered about the justification behind her warning: *"Avoid him! Avoid him!"* he heard her voice again and again as it reverberated on his mind above the whistling wind as it soughed as though trying to dislodge sequins from the block crepe sky.

"Here is the deal!" Kahuga persisted, cocking his head to the left. Muted, Agoyi simply stared into the depth of sky. "What would you say if I told you that I spoke to my buddies yesterday and they would like you to join our gang?"

"*Gang?*" a puzzled Agoyi said.

"Yeah! Our gang—the Haughty Boys! And mark my words, you will love it!"

"Me, join a *gang?*"

"Come-on, it is not that bad," he said in a coaxing tone.

"And what exactly do you do?"

"You have to join us in order to find out."

"No . . . I am not interested."

"At least give it some thought?"

Agoyi mumbled, indicating his displeasure, but Kahuga did not hear it.

"Alright then . . . why don't you think about it and then let me know. If you decide to join the group, meet me here tomorrow . . . same time."

"Phew!" Agoyi sighed in relief.

"Let us go home," Kahuga said rising-up. He offered Agoyi his right hand, which he grabbed as he hopped on his feet. The boys disembarked the rock, this time with less difficulty, for they simply slid down. Already, the sun had plunged into the same crack in the earth from which night time emerged.

"Let us meet tomorrow to finalize our plans," Kahuga said. "Right here!"

Agoyi did not respond. He was not contemplating joining Haughty Boys; instead, he was thinking about his grandmother. Would she be disappointed in him were she to know he was being recruited for a gang?

That evening, as the boys headed home, they barely spoke . . .

Chapter 11

That night, after Agoyi retired into his bed, he could barely sleep. His mind was troubled by two things: defying his grandmother and joining Haughty Boys. Disobeying her violated the Logooli people's moral code of respecting elders, but it affirmed his boyhood. So he lay in his bed, wondering what she would say were she to learn of his intentions. Would she force him to return to his father's home? Just thinking about it caused his body to shudder. He remembered how his stepmother had nearly killed him by stabbing. He also remembered his fight with Laban. He could not dare face another near peril experience.

In spite of his fears, the idea of belonging to a clique was very tantalizing. He thought of how lonely he would be were he to refuse joining the boys. Would he be a nobody? Or lonely as Kahuga had alleged?

"Perhaps membership to a gang might ease my transition into Ngoroke Village . . . just like Kahuga promised," he mumbled rolling in his bed.

"What would Guga say?" he had no idea.

Agoyi closed his eyes and thought some more about it, but was he ready to commit? 'Decisions! Decisions. Decisions!'

Agoyi mauled over this issue again and again and again. He flipped and flopped in his bed for hours. When sleep overtook him, he was on the verge of making-up his mind. Joining a gang was a chance of once in a life time . . .

Chapter 12

The next day, Kahuga was the first one to arrive on Lidaala as scheduled. Agoyi was not there. He promised to wait for him for only a half an hour. If he did not show-up on time, he would know he was not interested in joining Haughty Boys. As soon as he had ascended the rock, with some difficulty, he sat down and waited, eyeing the narrow footpath that led to the rock. There was nobody and no sound. Everything was still. In the stillness of it all, the air, every tree above the Hills, every sprig, every limb, every vine and every bloom appeared to have been bewitched into perfect immobility. He turned his eyes away from the hills and towards the river, gazing-up and down its winding banks. The water churned with a confused murmur, but there was not a soul in sight save for a reflection of the shimmering glimmer of light upon it. Slowly, he moved his eyes upwards into the depth of sky; it was clear pale-blue. No sign of rain save for hawks, sparrows, and woodpeckers that glided the skies. Then, he lowered his back onto the hard cold rock, closed his eyes, allowing his mind to be soothed by the humming of the Buhani River, the chirping of birds as they flew by, the whistling of the wind in every tree, every leaf, and every bough. He inhaled in the sweet scents of the wild flowers. All was peaceful. He was at peace, even. He who was greater than him knew he was at peace . . .

When Agoyi arrived an hour or so later, he did not hear him. Not even his huffing and puffing as he ascended the rock. He was simply startled from his temporary stupor when he felt a tapping on his left shoulder.

He jumped-up in fright as he saw an elongated shadow cast to the east. "Don't ever do that to me again, do you hear?" he said grumpily.

"Loud and clear! Agoyi said. "I didn't mean to frighten you. I am sorry," he said apologetically as he sat down Buddha style besides Kahuga.

There was silence. Kahuga closed his eyes. Agoyi stood-up and started pacing the rock. From time-to-time, he stole glances at Kahuga, who was pale faced. His hair was knotted, but concealed inside his signature red cap. His lips were dry and cracked. And his chest heaved up-and-down, up and down.

Agoyi moved his eyes from Kahuga to Buhani River in silence. The river hummed and its deep-blue waters calmly slithered towards Lake Victoria. Beyond the river, bare rocks of Maragoli Forest lay. He felt a cool drifting wind brush his exposed skin. He turned his eyes away from the river back to Kahuga. His eyes were shut, but he knew he was not sleeping. He turned his thoughts inward, wondering how he would break the news to him . . . Luckily, Kahuga reeled him back to his pulsing present:

"You finally decided to come," he said, without hiding his delight.

"I almost didn't."

"So what changed your mind?"

"I came to tell you that I won't join your gang."

"What?"

"You heard me . . . . I have decided not join the gang."

"You didn't have to waste your time and energy coming all the way here to tell me that," Kahuga said with a hint of irritation.

"It wasn't a waste of time!"

"And what do you call it?"

"Nothing. I didn't want you to speculate as to why I hadn't come."

"Your no show would have sufficed!"

"I preferred to do it in person."

"You've made your point. You can leave now," Kahuga said icily.

Agoyi did not move. He stood as still and straight as a soldier for inspection. He raised his head-up, rolling his eyes away from Kahuga. Nothing else moved. His body was immobile. His eyes now roved down to Buhani River. Its silent humming was soothing to his ear, but his mind percolated with a lot of doubts: had he made the right decision?

"You have made your point . . . You can go now."

Agoyi gasped, but said nothing.

He turned his eyes away from the river and back to kahuga. He was still laying on his back face-up. His eyes were gazing into the sky, but he did not see its clear pale-blue beauty.

"Alright then," Agoyi mumbled.

As he descended the rock, he felt Kahuga's eyes piercing his back.

"You'll be sorry for this! Kahuga barked.

Agoyi paused in his descend as though he was about to say something, but changed his mind. He neither turned nor muttered a word.

"Mark my words! You will be sorry."

Hurriedly, Agoyi descended the rock. Once his feet touched the ground, he paused and looked-up. He could still see Kahuga laying on the rock in the same position he had been when he arrived. From where he stood, Kahuga looked like a tiny spec on the giant rock. Agoyi turned his back away from the rock, away from Kahuga, and started walking home. At first, his gait was steady and calculated. Then, he increased pace, steadily and steadily and steadily. Before long, he was jogging up the narrow footpath. Soon, his jog was transformed into a run and running he did all the way home. Even when he stabbed his toes on stones in his path, or when pebbles pierced his soles, he did not pause to ease the throbbing pain from his feet. He ran like a mad man pursued by an invisible assailant. He did not stop until he was safely home—in his grandfather's compound. That was all there was to it . . .

Chapter 13

One afternoon, when he was on an errand to a nearby market, Agoyi had a scare of a lifetime. He walked out of the compound, along the narrow footpath towards the main road in high spirits. At the junction, he turned left, strolling eastward towards Ngoroke Primary School. Although school was not in session, standard eight students were present, attending tuition classes. He paused just for a moment ogling into the wide-open windows of the classroom. Countless heads of students peeped, though it was hard to distinguish the boys from girls. They all had neatly trimmed short hair, but their eyes were bright lit.

"Today, I want you to write me a composition!" he heard a teacher's robust voice say: "It has to be on something you have witnessed or experienced." A hushed murmur of confusion erupted.

"Yeah," Agoyi thought. *"There are many things I could write about."*

"Do you understand what that means?" the teacher queried.

"Yes teacher," the students responded almost in unison.

"Alright then, get to work!"

Agoyi turned his eyes away from the school to the shuffling sound of papers, away from the students and their teacher, away from everything he had hoped for, and dreamed about and desired during his formative life. He started walking mindlessly and slowly towards the bend in the road where the school compound ended. By the time he came around the corner, he could barely hear either the teacher or the students' voices. The class was beyond earshot and only a memory of his bygone days remained.

Thoughtlessly, he followed the road step-by-step. As he turned around the curve, he came headlong, bumping into Kahuga and his gang. They were three teenage boys. One of the boys wore a blue striped and short-sleeved shirt over a pair of navy blue shorts. He was the biggest one of the three and had the appearance of a ruffian. He would later learn his name was Chonjo, the Dispatcher. The other one was frail and lacked physical stature, but had an imposing gaze. He was wearing a white-short-sleeved shirt over a grey pair of pants—Ngoroke Primary school uniform. There was no way one could mistake Kahuga, for he had on his signature look: A shabby pair of blue jean shorts and a t-shirt. His hair looked unkempt, concealed behind his red cap, which he pushed over his ears, and a light brown-coloured jacket.

Agoyi was startled from his thought with Kahuga's robust voice, "There he is! That is the fool I told you about."

Flabbergasted, Agoyi stood still.

"What did I tell you?" Kahuga said taunting him.

Agoyi was soundless. The silence was barren, a muteness laced with acid.

"Speak-up boy . . . did someone cut your tongue?"

Agoyi neither moved nor muttered a word. He eyed him like a mute.

"I told you you'll be sorry! Didn't I? Ha?" he queried, poking Agoyi in his shoulder and pushing him towards the school fence.

Outnumbered, Agoyi remained befuddled.

Before he could collect his thoughts, before he could form a sentence, before he could open his lips to speak, the boys jumped him, giving him a thorough beating. They shoved him; they pushed him; they kicked him; and they punched him, as though he was a punch-bag.

Poor boy, he was too defenceless to resist the beating. Not wanting to give them the satisfaction, he silently vowed not to cry.

Someone shoved him again. He stumbled all the way to the ground. His posterior struck something sharp on the ground. A shockwave of pain crawled up his spine. He squealed, but showed no pain nor fear. He crawled along the fence like a baby, but remained soundless.

"Okay! He gets the point now," Kahuga said.

One of the boys kicked him once more.

"Okay, let him be," Kahuga said again.

The boys stopped.

"This is just a warning," he continued.

Agoyi was as quiet as rock and simply stared at him.

Kahuga took two steps towards him, but Agoyi did not move. He was immobile like a broken mill wheel.

Leaning towards him, inches away from his face, Kahuga said with a smirk on his face, "Now you know what to do . . . Tomorrow, meet me at our usual place or less next time you'll get double the dose . . ."

Agoyi gawked at him with bitter eyes and gritted his teeth. Although he was looking at him, he did not see him. His thoughts were distant—fixated to the time he and Kahuga had *fought*, to when he had been stabbed by his stepmother, to when he had a fight with Laban, and to when his father had uprooted him from home.

"Do you understand?"

Agoyi, still muted, simply gazed at him as the veins in his throat twitched nervously.

"These guys are ready to make your stay here a living hell. You can make that go away. . . You can make this go away! Do you understand?"

"Yes!" Agoyi said timidly.

"Tomorrow, be there! Got it?" he added, his voice dripping with arrogance.

"Crystal clear, sir!"

"Let us go!" Kahuga ordered the boys. They complied. Turning to Agoyi, he added: "Remember what I said."In a twinkling, the boys turned their backs away from him, walking around the bend heading west towards the village. They vanished as quickly as they had appeared, leaving a broken Agoyi to nurse his wounded pride.

Agoyi did not move. He simply sat by the roadside in mute silence.

The wind wrapped its fluid fingers around Agoyi's exposed skin gently and softly like a fluffed cotton ball. His eyes—wide open—gaped into the depth of sky; it was clear, pale-blue and imposing, but he was silent in his gazing. He saw nothing. Nearby, the wind whistled through the tree leaves along the fence like a train, but he was silent in his watching. He saw nothing. His grey feather-light shirt, fanned by gusting wind, ballooned and swayed around his body like a hot-air balloon, as though he were about to take flight, but he remained immobile save for his inner thoughts. Then a warm trickle snaked down his chin. He did not move a hand to wipe it off. The wind fanned it off his face, but he remained still, consumed in his gazing.

A draft passed, reeling Agoyi back to his pulsing present.

"What are you doing there?" he heard someone say.

"Nothing," he said, startled from his remembrance. He gathered himself up, dusted his clothes, and started walking slowly down the road continuing on his errand. Then, he burst out running all the way to the market and back . . .

Chapter 14

The next day, before Agoyi's met Kahuga at Lidaala, Ngoroke Village experienced one of the worst wind storms in its history. The squall was of great severity that it swept everything in its path. When it attained its utmost velocity, the air was thick with objects: clothes yanked from clothesline, rooftops lifted from unsecured mud huts; trees uprooted from the ground, and innumerable clothes and papers swept-up in the swirl were caught-up in twigs and boughs while some whirled around in the air and tossed back and forth and dropped upon the ground. The force of the wind was so strong that it even lifted a woman who was working on her farm off ground, tossed her up, as though she were feather light and then thrust her mangled body back to the ground in an awful thump. Her body jerked uncontrollably like a fish on a dock. No rains accompanied it, but it ushered in an interval of good storytelling.

As Agoyi walked out of his grandfather's compound, the wind storm had died down and a sudden calm returned to the village. The skies lightened cheerfully as though nothing had happened. As he walked, residual wind fiercely brushed his face, while his clothes flapped and floated around his body with ease like a butterfly. He had a difficult time keeping his eyes open, for the air was filled with dust particles. Warm tears snaked down the corners of his eyes, but he kept on walking. At the junction, he turned left heading towards Lidaala, the very place he and Kahuga had gone on his *initial* evening out. At the first turn, he veered towards the right. The pathway towards the stone snaked downwards through a shady meandering stony footpath. He had to fight shrubbery along the way, but careful enough not to bang his toes on the stones. He stooped constantly to avoid scratching his head on tree branches, but he pressed on. By the time he arrived at the gargantuan rock, the winds had quietened. He ascended it with ease only to find Kahuga awaiting his arrival.

"Have you made your decision?" Kahuga said, not giving him a moment of rest.

"To be honest, I don't believe I. . .," but before he could complete his thought, Kahuga interrupted him.

"So why are you here if you haven't made-up your mind?" he said with some irritation.

"I remembered something my grandfather had told me awhile ago."

"And what was that?"

"That a foolish man doesn't listen to his inner thoughts."

"He sounds like a very wise man!"

"Of course he is. Do you know something else he says?

"What?"

"All human beings are capable of making mistakes, but only fools persist in their errors."

"What is your point?

"I have made mistakes in the past!"

"So?"

"I am no fool!"

"So are you in or out?"

There was silence.

"Is this a one-time deal?"

"Are you in or out," Kahuga said again in a raspy voice, ignoring Agoyi's question.

"I don't have much choice in this matter, do I?" he mumbled.

"No!" Kahuga said nonchalantly, "Unless you want some more beating."

"I see!" A spell of silence followed.

"This time I might not be able to stop the boys like I did the yesterday."

"So what do we have to do?"

"Nothing crazy!"

"I see!"

"Let me take you on a small adventure tonight."

"What? Adventure? Tonight . . . You *mean* tonight?" Agoyi said befuddled.

"Uuh huh!"

"You're kidding me, right?"

"Nope!"

"I can't leave home at night!"

"Am sure you'll find away!" Kahuga said in a coaxing tone.

"But how?"

"Don't be a sissy! No one has to know about it."

"How can I leave home without my grandfather or grandmother knowing?"

"You *find* away!" Kahuga said coolly. "Just don't tell them about me . . . It'll be our little secret."

"A secret? I hate secrets."

"Then tell them the truth for all I care. See where that'll lead you!"

"I can't get in trouble with the Oldman . . . He is all I have." Kahuga did not respond. He just looked on. "I don't want to jeopardize my relationship with my folks. That is out of question."

"Suit yourself. Don't say you didn't know the consequence!"Kahuga said jabbing the fist of his right hand into his left.

Agoyi shrug his shoulders, but somewhat conflicted

with the thought of lying to his folks.

"It won't take long, only an hour tops! Your folks won't know you are gone. Trust me."

"When someone tells me *trust* me, I should have common sense to trust my conscience."

"You know what will happen if you did!"

"Don't remind me of that!" Agoyi said irritated, his mind flashing to the threat Kahuga had made earlier on, to how Kahuga and his boys had jumped him, giving him a thorough beating. He remembered how they shoved him , kicked him, and punched him.

"It is going to be very quick, you'll see," Kahuga said reassuringly.

"Let me think about it," Agoyi said as he reclined on the rock, closing his eyes in contemplation.

"Make it quick . . . I don't have all evening!" Kahuga said. Agoyi did not respond. A moment of silence elapsed between them.

"You don't want me to send those boys your way. Do you?" Kahuga added menacingly.

"Okay, just tonight!" Agoyi said reluctantly, even though he knew he was making a mistake, blackmailed in his decision. There was no turning back now. It was done. As a man of honour, he was fated to keep his word.

As he lay there, his mind took flight to the day everything changed in his life . . . It was a minor act: stealing his stepmother's money, but it came with greater consequences, not to mention the fight he had with Laban. Even though he felt *justified* in his action then, he was not *justified* in defying his grandmother. He knew and understood the difference between *right* and *wrong,* though amid the threats of blackmail and enjoying his boyhood, the two moral codes seemed muddled.

That night, the boys fixed to meet at the Oldman's gate and *that* was Agoyi's second act of *disobedience* . . .

Chapter 15

When Agoyi returned home, it was dark. The Oldman had already retired into the house, and his door was closed. As he got on the steps leading to the entrance door, he paused, turned in the direction he had come from, but there was nothing. He thought Kahuga was following him, but he had not. He heaved a sigh of relief, turning back to face the door. He did not mutter a word. Gently, he pushed the door open. The living room, in which the Oldman sat, was dimly lit by a *koroboi* lamp. A cool swift draft swept through the house nearly turning it off. Agoyi quietly pushed the door behind him. Slowly, and steadily, the lamp began to glow steadily again. Orange flames danced from its wick at a slight drift of wind. Small whiffs of smoke wafted upward and frizzled into empty space. The air inside was murky and smelt of nothing more, but kerosene fumes, a striking contrast to the freshness of the outside night air.

The Oldman was sitting in his fake red leather chair with his back buried deeply in its softness. His legs were crisscrossed and propped on his wooden stool. His eyes were closed as though forever shut in a state of eternal peace. His grey imposing eyebrows, thick like Kakamega rain forest, extruded on his dried chin as though untimely forced out. A weak smile loosely hung over his face. When he heard the door open, he mischievously lifted one of his eyelids, saw Agoyi approaching and forced it tightly shut, feigning to be asleep.

When Agoyi spotted the Oldman's *stiffened* body

slumped in his chair, he gasped: *'What a frightful sight!'*
A sinister thought cropped on his mind: 'What if the
Oldman were dead?' his body shuddered terribly at the
contemplation. *'Snap out of it!'* he mumbled, slapping
himself on one of his cheeks. He moved stealthily like
a thief towards the Oldman. When he reached him, he
leaned forward gaping into the Oldman's wrinkled face,
but he was as stiff as a log. He almost touched his bushy
eyebrows, but refrained himself. Another bad thought
flashed his mind: *'He is dead.'*

Bravely, he poked the Oldman's shoulder. He did not
move a muscle. He remained soundless and immobile.
Not wanting to give up, he touched his neck; his body
was warm. 'Phew!" he gasped. 'He has to be asleep!'
He turned away from the Oldman, took a chair by the
entrance and sat down, wondering what would happen
to him were the Oldman to die unexpectedly. Would his
father come for him?

Next, he feigned a cough, hoping to awaken the Oldman
from his stupor, but he remained sullenly still.

He coughed again and waited. Nothing happened. He
coughed a third time. The Oldman moved, and his chair
creaked. Agoyi sighed in relief as he pushed the whole
idea of his grandfather being dead from his mind.

"*Guga*—grandfather," he mumbled weakly. "V*wakiila!*"
That was the only right thing to say during such an
awkward moment.

Instead of responding to Agoyi's evening greeting, the
Oldman coughed, clearing his throat. Grumpily, he said,
"What is it that you want, poking me in my shoulder like
that?"

"Nothing," he said plainly. "I just thought . . . Eeh,
perhaps, something was wrong with you. . . I am sorry if
I disturbed you." Agoyi said apologetically not wanting to
overextend the conversation.

"That is alright . . . Whisper in my ear next time."

Agoyi nodded in agreement."Alright *Guga!*" he added.

"And where are you coming from this late?"

"I had just gone to walk around the village."

"You should be careful when you are out there. Do you know we have many hooligans in this village? Be on the look-out for these riffraff. If they threaten you in any way," he paused, "You let me know . . . alright."

"Yes *Guga!*"

Not much transpired between the two men after that. The Oldman sat quietly in his chair. His eyes remained shut. As for Agoyi, his mind was at bay. He wondered if his grandfather already knew about his activities. Perhaps, he had a second sense about these things? So he pushed his back into the crown of his chair, closed his eyes anticipating his grandmother's cooking.

The sun had already set when Agoyi's grandmother brought supper onto the table, but his mind was already distracted with his impending outing. In his distraction, he forgot proper social etiquette his family observed at every meal: to bless the meal. No sooner had his grandmother set the food on the table than he reached out for the spoon and served himself. He almost ate before the Oldman had blessed the meal, but one stern look from his grandmother halted his tomfoolery. He dropped his eyes to the ground in embarrassment, for he understood his mistake right away.

"Agoyi," his grandmother said with a smile. He lifted his head in shame, afraid to meet her disapproving gaze. "Why don't you bless the food?" she added in a soft low broken voice.

Agoyi had never blessed a meal his entire life and did not know what to do. He looked at his grandmother and then at the Oldman, as though he was begging them not to make him do it. They did not say anything, but returned his gaze. His grandmother closed her eyes. The Oldman closed his eyes. An awkward moment of silence elapsed between them. Agoyi closed his eyes too, but in cowardice . . . How could he tell them he did not know how to pray?

To save the day, the Oldman said, "Let us pray!"

Agoyi pushed one of his eyelids open looking at the Oldman. His face was expressionless, but both his eyes were shut. On his forehead, his bushy eyebrows protruded. He moved his open eye from the Oldman to his grandmother. Her eyes were tightly shut in reverence. He could see the signs of her aging on her forehead. Furrowed lines crawled from her left temple to her right. Then he shifted his gaze across the table. He wondered what would have happened had a cat been in the house. He imagined it pouncing on the beef stew serving bowl, just to steal a piece of meat, or flipping it over, spilling its entire contents. He wondered if he would dive to save the stew from spilling all over the floor were that to happen. He aborted that idea knowing he could be burnt in the process. Perhaps be scarred for life. That would be tragic. He forced these thoughts out of his mind as the Oldman began to pray.

"Oh God bless this food before we take it for the nourishment of our bodies. Amen!" It was a short and simple prayer. As he mumbled the word 'Amen,' Agoyi pushed his eyelids shut lest his grandfather know he had one eye open the entire time. He kept his eyes closed until he heard the clamouring sounds of spoons against his grandmother's metallic serving bowls.

"You can open your eyes now," she said with a mysterious smile on her face.

"Yes Guku," Agoyi said. Mutely, he watched the Oldman as he took a generous serving of *ugali, sukuma wiki,* and beef stew. His eyes bulged out as the savoury aroma of food wafted his way, making his mouth water. He could almost taste the delectable *Simba Mbili* curry powder, fresh garlic and cilantro, but he would not dare reach for the food until it was his turn. He sat and waited patiently. Among Logooli people, old folks have the right to serve first, followed by the children and mothers are last . . . That was the Logooli way.

When it was his turn, he hurriedly heaped a mountain of food on his plate like a *chokora* boy. His grandmother looked at him with an expression which reminded him that there was plenty of food for everyone. There was no need for him to act in a gluttonous manner. He understood her unspoken words, but that did not stop him from hogging his food hurriedly. He knew he did not have much time left before Kahuga made a showing at the gate, a place they had agreed to meet that night.

"Guku," he said after he had eaten to his fill, "Thank you very much. Your food is very delicious," he said licking his fingers. She smiled broadly. Agoyi knew how to flatter the old lady. The art of flattery, when least expected, was like nectar to her ears. And he exploited it to the fullest. Her food defined her womanhood. The Oldman and Agoyi did not have to say anything . . . Their generous serving was testament enough. She felt rewarded for their sheer enjoyment of her cooking. Her warm smile and the glitter in her big round eyes were sufficient. That made Agoyi feel guilty for yielding to Kahuga's pressure. Nevertheless, the remote thrill of being inducted into the band of the Haughty Boys of Ngoroke made him forget any guilt he might have felt.

When Agoyi left his grandfather's house after supper, the night was still young. Countless stars glinted in the big dipper like tiny polka dots, showering the dark clear sky. And the air was not only pitilessly raw, but also much colder than he had anticipated. His body shuddered slightly in its chilliness. Suddenly, he wished he had not agreed to go out that night, but he knew he had no choice. He made a reluctant promise to kahuga and a promise made is a debt unpaid. So he had good memory to keep it. As any man, he would not dare to go back on his word. That was what a real man did.

He did not walk to his hut right away. He stood there, in the middle of the compound, stiff like a board. The very spot he had stood when his grandmother warned him against keeping company with Kahuga. Suddenly, he became consumed with fear, a mind-blogging fear. It was a fear of betrayal. He wondered what she would say if she knew. Would she send him back to his father and step-mother? His body shivered at that thought.

Just as he was about to take his first step towards his hut, he heard movement. He froze mid-step. A chill crawled up and down his spine like icicles. He opened ears as wide as his eyes, even though he could not see in the dark. He wished he had been gifted with bat eyes that could see in darkness. His fears subsided as he realized the movement was caused by a passer-by along the road. *"Phew!"* he gasped, relieved that it was not a leopard or a night-runner.

Without thinking, he dashed into his hut and pushed the door shut. He resolved to stay there until Kahuga came for him. Without doubt, he was certain he would, and he was right. After a couple of minutes, he heard a voice from outside.

"Psst! Psst! Agoyi!"

Agoyi walked to the window, pushed his head on the hard cold glassy surface and peered through it, but it as too dark for him to see.

"Psst! Psst! Agoyi . . . Are you in there?"

"Kahuga! Is that you?"

"Yes, hurry up will you?"

"Be right there!"

Agoyi ran into his bedroom and took his spotlight.

He dashed out, pulling the door behind him as quietly as he could. He snuck out of the compound through the back fence. He was careful enough not to puncture his skin during the process. Once he was safely out of the compound, the two boys walked in silence following the same footpath to the junction where the road forked. This time, they turned right, heading westwards towards the steep hills which led to Mung'oma caves. They climbed up the embankment in silence, past the village shop, until they came to its pinnacle and stopped. Below them, Ngoroke village had the appearance of a soundly sleeping giant. In the absence of electricity, home owners remained in perpetual darkness, hardly a surprising truth. A few homes had a glint of light, while most were invisible in this impenetrable darkness. Kahuga knew it was only a matter of minutes before the entire village would be sound asleep.

"Let us wait here for awhile," Kahuga said.

"Why?"

"Don't ask many questions."

"How long shall we have to wait?" Agoyi scowled.

"Just until Desi and Keya turn their lights off."Desi and Keya were an elderly couple that lived at the base of the hill.

"What is your plan?"

"I'll tell you once we get there."

The boys stood stalk still, watching the sleeping giant like hawks. Nothing else transpired between them save for an occasional drifting wind. They were like two flittering ghosts in the night. Had anyone seen them, they could have easily been mistaken for night-runners.

Without a word to his friend, Agoyi shuffled his feet sideways like a blind man looking for a place to sit. Kahuga followed suit. Their eyes peered through darkness below them to the *almost* sleeping giant. A cool draft passed bringing a chill to Agoyi's body. Within no time, he began to complain about being cold.

"It is getting colder!"

"Yeah . . . I know."

"When are we going to begin the adventure?"

"In a little while."

"And when is that?"

"Shut-up, will you? You can't rush a good thing."

Agoyi's eyes roved the hill—sideways, up and down—but it was useless. He could not see much.

"Agoyi," Kahuga gasped with enthusiasm. "Look down yonder!"

"Where?"

"At those houses in the valley."

"Which ones?"

"To the right and at the base of the hill."

Agoyi peered through the darkness, struggling to see.

"Do you see them? The only houses with lights on."

Agoyi took a second glance and it was with great difficulty that he noticed them.

"What do you want with them?" he queried.

"Nothing now, but once the lights are out, we can move."

Then, there was silence again as the boys kept a vigilant watch of the houses.

"We don't want both, just the smaller house," Kahuga said, breaking the silence between them.

"I see."

"The compound with the bigger house has a very giant dog. If we go there, we'll be handing ourselves to *Iliigutu*." So the boys continued their watch of the houses in silence.

Moments later, it was Kahuga who spoke. "Do you know what he might do to us?"

"Who?"

"*Iliigutu,* the village adjudicator?"

"What might he want with us?"

"If he caught us, you know!"

"What are you talking about?"

Ignoring Agoyi, Kahuga noted, "He might whisk our bottoms with his leather belt. Wham Bum! His lashes might be so ruthless we might not have any use of them for a very long time. He might cuff our hands/handcuff us, throw us in a Landover, and drive us to Vihiga Police Station."

"What are you talking about?" Agoyi said again.

"Once we go down there . . . Who knows what might happen?"

"I am out of here," Agoyi said staggering up, wanting to go back home. "Count me out!"

"Am just making conversation," Kahuga said reassuringly. "We won't get caught?"

Agoyi did not understand.

"Don't forget why you are here?" Kahuga added threateningly.

"What choice do I have?" Agoyi said, hating himself.

"Mind you, this is just a trial."

"I am regretting this already!"

"Hey my friend!" dismissing Agoyi's comment. "It seems we are in business afterall."

"What?"

"The lights!"

"Look!"

"Where?"

"There . . . at Desi's . . . they are out!"

"The house with the dog?"

"No, don't be silly . . . the smaller house."

"What about the dog?" Agoyi said nervously.

"It doesn't trespass! It is always on a leash."

"Are you sure about that?"

"Yes I am sure," Kahuga said. "Let us go," he added.

"Are you sure you are ready for this?" Agoyi said, a sudden fear enveloping him.

"Uuh!" Kahuga said. Quietly, the boys rose from where they had been sitting and started heading southwards. Everything around them was soundless. Only their hearts thumped loudly and rapidly that they could hear each other's breathing. Their feet moved robotically.

Distantly and intermittently, they could hear sounds of chirping crickets. They moved stealthily like thieves in the night, not wanting to awaken those already under the hands of slumber. A couple of times, they bumped into drunkards who hobbled along the footpath in a drunken stupor. It was not difficult to avoid them because they were not only loud, but also sung as they staggered along. One drunkard kept on spewing filth against his neighbour, but the boys ignored.

The boys thrust their feet forward gently and carefully like men walking on stilts. They tip-toed along a narrow footpath among grown shrubbery and boulders, bending their heads from time to time trying to avoid being scratched on their heads by twigs. At times, they would crawl on their bottoms out of fear of falling down and injuring themselves. Save for Agoyi, Kahuga was very familiar with the terrain. He knew if they were to missa step, people would scrape their remains from the bottom of the hill. So, he led the way and Agoyi followed.

"I wish the moon was out," Agoyi said, breaking the creeping silence between them.

"A moon is a sign of bad luck," Kahuga said as the boys continued their descent of the hill.

A twig snapped behind them.

"Wait a minute," Agoyi said nervously. The boys stopped to listen.

"Did you hear that?"

"No!" Kahuga said with a hint of irritation.

"Never mind! It is probably a stray cat . . ." Agoyi said.

"Let us go!" Kahuga said.

"Alright!"

The boys walked in silence, past the big house. The dogs did not bark. They were now approaching the gate to Desi and Keya's compound. The closer they drew to it, the more nervous Agoyi became.

Once at the gate, they investigated the home, but it was too dark for them to see much. Convinced they were safe, they snuck into the compound like prowlers.

"Let us check the bedroom window first," Kahuga advised. Slowly, and carefully, to avoid detection, they crept to the back of the house on their hands and knees.

"This is it," Kahuga whispered to Agoyi. He moved his left ear to the window to listen. The house was as still as a cemetery, besides the heavy breathing of the couple inside.

"I don't hear anything," he mumbled. "They must be asleep."

"Don't you think we should wait a little?"

"What difference would it make if they were already asleep?"

"I guess none!"

Kahuga peeped into the house through the giant cracks of the window. The inside was just as dark as the outside. Convinced this was the right time for them to stage their attack, Kahuga said, "We have to use the backdoor."

"Are you sure about this?" Agoyi said.

"Yes, I am sure," he remarked affirmatively. "I know this house like I know my own house."

"What are we looking for?" Agoyi queried.

"You'll see in a minute."

The boys crept to the back of the house. The door was not strong because it had been poorly constructed by a local *jua kali*—whose workmanship left a lot to be desired. Kahuga was aware of that truth, for he had been in the house many times.

No sooner had they got to the back than they stopped to listen again. They had to be careful or risk being caught. Kahuga reached in his jacket and pulled out a penknife.

"Did you remember to bring the spotlight?"

"Yes!"

"Let me have it!"

Agoyi rammed his right hand inside the jacket and fished out a spotlight. Just as he was about to hand it to Kahuga, they heard a loud hooting sound of an owl; it was followed closely by a startling commotion, much like a scuffle.

"Listen! Don't make any sound," Kahuga advised.

Right away, Agoyi felt dizzy as though the ground upon which he stood was spinning. His feet jelled from under him as he collapsed on the ground. His torch rolled out of his hand. The scuffling sound increased, and Agoyi's body hit the ground with an awful thud.

Confused as to whether he should run for his life or attend to his friend, Kahuga stood still. Before these new developments, they were supposed to go into the couple's house, sweep it clean, and run out. It was that simple. Nothing more, nothing less! Call it a twist of fate. Now, he had to contend with the truth that his *friend* may have suffered a heart attack. He wanted to run, but he could not. Instead, he leaned forward towards his body and touched one of the veins on his neck. He could feel his pulse.

"He is not dead!" he whispered more to himself than anyone else. "Snap out of it," he muttered into Agoyi's ear, tapping gently on one of his cheeks.

Concomitantly, the scuffling noises on the other side of the house continued and increased in intensity. Once again, and, for a split second, Kahuga contemplated aborting their heist, abandoning Agoyi, but changed his mind as quickly as he had thought of it. No, he could not leave him there.

"What are you doing slapping me?" Agoyi grumbled as he emerged from a temporary lapse of memory.

"Because you had me scared stupid . . . . That is why."

"What happened?" Agoyi said, staggering-up.

"You passed out . . . that is what happened. You passed out!"

"Did not," Agoyi protested bitterly.

"Did too!"

As he steadied himself, he knocked his spotlight, which had fallen to the ground at his collapse. He bent down and picked it. Meanwhile, the scuffling continued.

No sooner had Agoyi fully regained consciousness than the boys scuttled into a clump of bananas near the house.

"Quick, run!" Kahuga said. Agoyi was already on his heels before Kahuga had finished his remark.

Once safely hiding behind a cluster of bananas, the boys sat quietly and patiently, waiting for the scuffle to die down. It did not, it continued on and on and on, only this time, it was accompanied by a growling sound.

"Let me have the light," Kahuga whispered. Agoyi handed him the light, but still felt very fretful.

"Stay here!" Kahuga commanded.

Scared to be left alone and in the dark, Agoyi said, "No! I want to come too!"

"Suit yourself!" Kahuga said.

Like somnambulists, the boys walked furtively and stopping every so often towards the direction of the scuffle. Each boy took short and deep breaths as they came within earshot of the noise. They stopped abruptly. Kahuga took a long prolonged sigh. Agoyi heaved out of fear. Without thinking, Kahuga flipped the switch on the spotlight in the direction of the scuffle.

When they saw what it was: Two dogs stuck together; the boys burst out in muffled laughter. Unable to control themselves, they laughed and laughed until tears glided down their cheeks. When it all subsided, they felt a deep sense of relief, knowing that their fears were unfounded. They also knew the two creatures could not do them any harm. Common sense told them the dogs were destined to be in that position for a very long time.

Agoyi vouched to tell his friends back home, of how he had been frightened almost to death by two dogs stuck together. He knew they would laugh at him for days. Turning to Kahuga, he mumbled something about continuing with what had brought them to Desi's home. Kahuga complied.

The boys returned to Desi's back door without incident. They were careful enough not to attempt any break in without listening to the rhythmic breathing sounds of those within. They heard someone snoring, and that was a good sign.

Fishing for his knife from his pocket, Kahuga pushed it between the door and the guardrail. He heard a snapping sound.

"We've made it!" he whispered triumphantly. Gently, he pushed the door inside; it creaked slightly. They heard someone stir in the bedroom. The boys stopped to listen.

No one moved. The boys took their first steps into the house and then stopped to listen. There was no sound. They waited for a second before making their next move. Nothing happened. Gently, Kahuga pushed the door behind them. It made a loud screeching sound, startling the couple. Their ducks, which slept in the kitchen, started quacking. They heard someone hurriedly jumping out of bed. Kahuga knew it had to be Keya who knew ducks never quack, unless there was an intruder in the home.

"Who is there?" Keya shouted.

There was a ginormous silence.

"Shhh!" Kahuga said.

"Who is there?" Keya said once more. There was no answer, just silence.

The boys stood still as though they had been transformed into fossils in a museum.

"Who is there?" Keya said again, his voice trembling with fear.

The boys remained muted in the hallway next to the kitchen door.

Noisily, Keya felt his way from the bedroom towards his backdoor, coming within inches of the boys. The boys held their breath. Quick thinking, Kahuga flipped the switch on the spotlight and dashed for the kitchen. He grabbed the nearest five-pound bag of grain and scurried back out. Agoyi felt a familiar dizziness return to him, but he battled it as he bolted out of the house behind Kahuga. The boys stole behind the clump of bananas. There, they could hear the dogs scuffling. They could also still hear Keya fumbling with the door, afraid his hand would wrench it open. He did not; instead, he locked it, for it was pointless for him to walk into the dark in his blindness.

Meanwhile, when Desi felt the rushed manner with which Keya had sprung out of bed, she knew something was terribly wrong. Startled, she fumbled for a matchbox to light her *koroboi* lamp. She knocked over the lamp in the process. Afraid its kerosene might spill, she hurriedly, searched for her matchbox. When she found it, she picked it, pulled it open, took a matchstick and with one strike, it bursted into flames. She used it to locate her lamp, which was tilted near the edge of her bed. She ignited it. The room became engulfed by strong kerosene fumes.

Quickly, she stormed out of the bedroom heading towards the backdoor, but she was too late. The boys had already made their expeditious exit from the house. She only saw the door flying back into place and next to it, was Keya sweeping the floor with his hands trying to locate the stick he used to lock the door. Desi walked to him, picked the half-broken stick and handed it to him. There was nothing odd or unusual about it. She concluded the old man must have had an urgent call of nature. She turned back and walked into the bedroom as though nothing had happened.

Keya locked the door, pressing his ear to it. He listened as the footsteps of his intruders scuffled off until they died down. He, too, like his wife, went back to bed. Unlike his wife, he could not push what had just happened out of his mind. He was certain someone had been in his house. That fact was clear, but he could not tell his wife about it, not until morning. Inwardly, he knew that if only he had had the eyes to see and his wife the ears to hear, they could have caught their assailants . . .

Long after the storm of their near capture had quieted, the boys sat in the clump of bananas for a very long time, chatting about their narrow escape.

The dogs, which had startled them earlier on, had dislodged and were busy playing catch with each other.

"Chui! Chui! Chui!" Kahuga called one of the dogs. "*Kuja hapa*—come here*!*" he bellowed. The dog growled as it advanced towards the boys, wagging its tail. Its female counterpart lagged behind, but followed very closely.

No sooner had Chui reached where the boys were than Kahuga extended his right hand towards him. Chui growled at him, licking his hand playfully.

"*Kwenda huko!*" he barked at Chui after he had got tired of his slobbery lick, chasing him away. Chui did not hover around after being chased away, but with his tail folded between his legs, he scuttled. The boys listened to the dogs chasing each other in play until their sounds died down.

Later, the boys walked out of the banana plantation, with Kahuga dragging their loot in his right hand. Since it was dark, and, granted, he knew his grandfather would not awaken until the crack of dawn, he placed the sack on the steps of his *isiimba*—hut.

The boys lay down on the cold dew laden grass. Its chillness did not matter to them, particularly, Kahuga who felt elated about their accomplishment. Little shrieks and currents of laughter ruptured between them. It was a magical moment of their colossal triumph. Kahuga boasted about the robbery, but Agoyi was uncomfortable about the whole affair. He complained about how unjust life could be. Though they had not been caught, but he still felt as though he had. He had just participated in something that conflicted with his moral beliefs. There was no justification for it beyond the thrill of being mischievous. He remembered what his father had told him in his hospital bed, *"Stealing was stealing, and it was wrong. That was all there was to it! . . ."*

Laying on the grass, each boy withdrew into his inner self, his eyes leering into the gigantic night sky mesmerized by its grandeur. It was pitch-black save for a band of the Milky Way, which like a fuzzy light stretched endlessly on the further away horizon. Not to mention the stars and these glinted above them like polka dots.

Agoyi intimated that one of those stars had to be his mother watching over him:

"If only she could see me now, she would be mighty disappointed. I am not that perfect child a mother wishes for," he mumbled sadly.

"Perhaps," Kahuga said, pausing briefly. Then on second thought, he added, "But . . . Come to think of it, had she been alive, you wouldn't have been here. Our paths may never have crossed. And, mostly, what happened tonight may have not occurred at all."

"I guess you are right!" Agoyi remarked.

So the boys lay there for a very long time, until they completely lost track of time. When Agoyi left for home, it was after midnight. On his back, he dragged the bag of grain, which Kahuga had lifted from Keya's home . . .

Chapter 16

At dawn, even before the voice of Irene, the village recluse, pierced the morning daybreak in prayer, or even before the roosters had crowed to summon dawn, Keya awoke to the shrill screams of his wife. Already, the landscape was shrouded in a grey mist through which occasional raindrops fell.

"*Wui*! What happened here?" he heard her say distantly.

"*Wui* Keya! What happened here?"

Startled from his sleep, Keya hopped out of bed and started feeling his way to the kitchen. The wailing of his wife reminded him of what happened the previous night: They were robbed.

"What is going on here?" he said, struggling to find his way to the kitchen.

Desi did not hear him; instead, she kept on saying frantically, "I can't see my maize! I can't see my maize!" She flung her arms wide open, let them fall on her body, and then stood still with an unmoved face and stony eyes. And that nagged Keya to his wits end.

Desi was an early riser. She preferred to complete her morning chores before the sun was perfectly balanced above the sky. After completing her chores, she enjoyed spending the remainder of her day sitting under a tree shade preparing her evening meal: plucking her vegetables, *imiito, ilikuvi, zisaaga,* or any other vegetable in her possession. That was her life, much like every woman in Ngoroke. When she got tired, or if she did not have much to do in the day, she took pleasure relaxing under the canopy of a tree or until it was time for her to begin preparing supper.

That was not the case that morning. No sooner had she got into the kitchen to begin her chores than she realized she had been robbed. Right there, in the middle of her kitchen, she stood with her hands akimbo, stupefied and angry. She kept on questioning her husband:

"Who does that?"

Keya had no answer, for he was still finding his way to the kitchen.

"Keya, what shall we do? All our maize is gone . . . all of it. Five *gorogoro!* There is nothing left," she said despondently.

"Why couldn't they take one or two *gorogoro*? Those wretched souls!"

She stood there, right there in her kitchen. Dismayed. Bewildered. She threw her hands in the air, mumbling something to herself, "I know I left it here before I went to bed!" She paced the floor befuddled. She moved her right hand to her chin, her index finger touching her lower lip. And with her eyes still making a thorough sweep of her kitchen again, she mumbled: "Yeah! It was definitely here. Right here alright! . . . I must be losing my mind too," she added just as Keya stumbled into the room, his hands pressed against the wall, which he used as a guide.

"Eeh! Desi," he said, but his wife was as deaf and hard of hearing as the grey monitor lizard. "Remember last night . . . well . . . eeh . . . when you walked in . . ." he fumbled with an opening to tell his wife they had been robbed the previous night, but she already knew it. He gave-up trying. Communication between them had become unbearable ever since she lost her hearing, too much of a struggle.

"Keya . . . *Avasweta!*" she exclaimed. "I know I left it here." Dumbfounded, she sat on her kitchen floor, a defeated dumb.

Sensing his wife's distraught state, Keya mumbled: "If only Desi knew how to read, I could have explained it to her that way." Even so, she never had an education, for her father believed it was a waste to educate girls. That was 1932. The only thing a girl could do was to get married.

"Perhaps Kahuga knows something," he murmured, walking outside the house.

Although the sun was up, it exuded no heat and the air was cool and nippy.

He walked out of the house, into the drizzles of rain, all the way to the boy's door. He gently tapped on it. There was no response. He tapped on it again and again and again. There was no answer.

Then, he called out his name.

There was no answer. Keya waited for a second.

"Kahuga," again, there was no answer.

"Kahuga!" he said for the fifth or sixth time.

"Yes *Guga!*" he heard the boy's aggravated voice from inside.

"Could you come out right away?" Keya said, with a quiver in his voice.

"Yes *Guga.*"

Keya stood outside, in the mist waiting for his grandson. He heard his footsteps from inside as a hand wrenched open the door. He emerged bare chested, holding his shirt in his right hand.

"We got robbed last night," Keya said.

"What are you talking about? We . . . robbed?" Kahuga said in disbelief, putting on his shirt to shield himself from the drizzles.

"Yes, someone robbed us last night."

"Really!"

"In deed . . . I heard them, but they were too quick for me."

"Did *Guku* see them?"

"If she had, I wouldn't be asking or would I?"

"I am sorry *Guga.* I didn't hear a thing . . . I must have slept deep through it like death."

"You mean to say you didn't even hear the dogs?"

"Not even a sound . . . nothing. I must have been dead asleep!"

"Someone stole your grandmother's maize!"

"Oh my goodness, you don't say!"

"Oh, yes!"

"Who can do such a thing to *Guku*? May the culprit be punished ten-fold!"

"So, you didn't hear a thing!"

"Nope! Don't know anything about it!"

"I see!" Keya said, walking away from his grandson and back to his house. He was soaking wet.

Kahuga watched him nervously as his mind took flight to the day he had attempted to steal his grandfather's ewe. That was long ago. It backfired. The punishment he received then was enough to bring him back to his senses. Or had it? He thought Keya suspected him, but amid all the suspicion, he knew it, too, shall pass . . .

Chapter 17

At Oldman's home, no one could have guessed Agoyi had joined Kahuga's gang, a marauding band of thugs. His life progressed steadily and with ease. He did his chores as was expected. He showed respect to his folks. Whenever sent on an errand, he went without question. He was the epitome of goodness; the Oldman and his grandmother were both proud of him. He was handsome and pleasant in every way: short, dark skinned, bright faced with a charming radiant smile. Whenever he smiled, he exposed his chalk-white teeth, which gleamed as though bleached daily to maintain an impeccable radiance.

Unlike Agoyi, there was very little good one could say about Kahuga save for his free-spirited nature. He was snobbish. That was clear. His nose and his scrawny cheeks showed signs of malnourishment. One look at him, anyone with good moral judgment avoided him like a plague. He was malicious, capricious, and manipulative. He never combed his hair, a poor excuse for dreadlocks, which he stuffed under a red cap and pushed it over his ears. He also wore a light-brown jacket. He walked with his eyes lowered onto the ground and hands into his pockets. Whether it rained or not, he wore it. Astute mothers advised their sons to stay away from him. Unfortunately, some boys were drawn to his irresistible free spirit, while others found themselves in his company by entrapment.

He founded Haughty Boys to keep boys out of trouble, but soon it morphed into a band of thugs without a conscience that terrorized the community for sheer excitement. There were two distinct sets: the scouts and the dispatchers. Scouts scampered the village for stuff, while dispatchers sold everything the scouts brought. Kahuga was the kingpin and had recently recruited Agoyi as a new scout for a *major* job, a truth concealed from him. He neglected to tell him that the boys only terrorized those close of kin to them. No one knows why they did it; they simply did it. Perhaps, it was the thrill they derived from it that they coveted . . .

Chapter 18

That same morning after the robbery, Kahuga did not waste time, but visited Agoyi at home. Already, the rain had subsided and the sun shone brilliantly above the Hills. It was the first time he had been bold enough to walk into the Oldman's compound. He had seen him heading towards the *baraza*, a formal meeting ground, where elders learned of the village's happenings. He was certain the *baraza* was going to discuss the robbery at Keya's home. Fortunately, without a shred of evidence to implicate the perpetrator, Keya had no case. Just another lost case and he knew it only too well.

Upon his arrival, Kahuga marched into Agoyi's hut, but it was empty.

"Agoyi! Agoyi?" he called out his name.

"Who is there?" he heard Agoyi say from inside the pen.

"It is me, Kahuga."

"In here!"

Kahuga walked fast towards the pen. He forced the door open. He spotted Agoyi cleaning the stall. His hands were covered with dung. Kahuga broke into a derisive laughter, but Agoyi ignored him.

Right away, Agoyi remembered his grandmother's warning against Kahuga, but it was too late. He had already overlooked her warning.

Soon, curiosity got the better part of him. He wanted to know what had happened when Keya woke-up to realize he had been robbed.

"What did Keya say about it?" Agoyi asked excitedly.

"He asked me if I had heard anything,"

"What did you say?"

"What do you think I said . . . nothing of course!"

"He doesn't suspect you . . . he doesn't suspect us, or does he?"

"Not a thing!" Kahuga said boisterously.

"You sly dog! Can we get away with it?"

"Of course we will!" Unbeknownst to Agoyi, this was not the first-time Kahuga had stolen from his grandparents. It had all begun innocently with him taking an egg from his grandmother's chicken coop, which he exchanged for *mandazi* or *simsim* and peaked when he stole an ewe.

"As long as we can keep a low profile for a couple of days, we should be okay."

"What do you want me to do with *it*?"

"Keep *it* safely for now. I will tell you later after I speak to Chonjo, the Dispatcher!"

"Who is he?"

"The person who disposes all our merchandise. You will meet him soon."

"All right then!"

Kahuga was just about to go when he remembered something: "By the way, don't forget our other little arrangement. The other one was a total burst!" he said with a giggle.

"Don't push your luck. Make sure my grandmother doesn't see you on your way out. You might land me into deep trouble."

"Later . . ." he said, pulling open the door to the pen. He peeped outside for a second. "Cause clear!" he added as he walked out. The door fell back into its place. Agoyi watched it until it came to a standstill before he continued with his morning chore. After milking the cows, he had one more chore: to cut napier grass to feed the cows . . .

Chapter 19

The night the boys began planning their biggest heist, Agoyi ate his supper hurriedly. That was a week after their 'heist' at Keya's home. His mind seethed with fear, but also excitement, for he had decided to be one with the boys. He felt it was something much greater than he had initially thought. The group gave him security. It gave him a sense of purpose. It made him forget his previous trouble with his stepmother. It gave him thrills. What more could he have asked for? He even fooled himself that Ngoroke was by far much better than Bute Village. He wondered why he had been angry with his father for plucking him from his home.

Even though he had agreed to temporarily join a roguish gang, it was not something for which he was proud. He knew his grandmother would disapprove; and that instilled fear in him. As for his father, he did not care what he thought. He was the very reason he had left Bute. Though what troubled him most was rejection. What if the other boys did not like him? What would he do? Would he lead a lonely life in Ngoroke? He was nervous about meeting Chonjo, the Dispatcher. He was nervous about meeting the rest of the gang, and that was just that: jitters of a boy seeking acceptance.

The sun had gone down when Agoyi walked to his hut, took his spotlight and snuck out of the compound through the back. It was his second . . . No, his third time. He made sure the Oldman, and his grandmother had not seen him leave. As always, he crept through the fence and ran towards the gate. Kahuga was awaiting his arrival as he routinely did. The boys walked towards Mung'oma Caves until they reached its summit to a rock, as flat as a discus, which Kahuga and the boys designated as a good meeting ground. Once there, they sat down and started planning what to do with their loot from Keya. All the while, they sat in wait of Chonjo, the Dispatcher's arrival.

"Chonjo will pick-up the merchandise tonight," Kahuga said.

"That is fine . . . the sooner, the better."

"He has to sell it off tomorrow."

"No problem."

"We will split the profit afterwards."

"How do we know he won't defraud us?" Agoyi queried.

"He won't! He can't con a conman," Kahuga said.

"Phew! That makes me feel good." Though inwardly, he could not help, but wonder if both Chonjo and Kahuga would not dupe him.

"Mind you, I won't be far from him. He will handle the transaction, while I watch from the peripheral. That is how we do it." Kahuga was careful about that and none of his dispatchers has ever double-crossed him. The penalty for breaching that trust was so severe no dispatcher dared to break it: Flogging was the punishment the boys inflicted upon each other for disloyalty.

The boys deliberated and planned their next heist. It was a monumental job. If they succeeded, it would be their biggest job ever. They hoped to execute it perfectly. A repeat of what happened at Keya's was out of the question. Plans for their next heist would take several days. No one was exempted from participation, not even Agoyi. His involvement guaranteed him permanent membership into the gang.

The night was dark and the air cool and comfortable, and the boys, who had transformed themselves into nocturnal creatures, sat in silence. They were at peace, soaking in the chirping sounds of crickets and croaking frogs. They drew into their lungs the clear air. There, at the pinnacle of the hill, the boys appeared like two lovers, watching the sleeping village with killer eyes . . . No, a robber's eyes. Behind them, stood a towering guava tree; its every branch, its enormous leaves swayed in drifting wind. Sporadically, their eyes darted furtively from the tree into the vast vacant sky with its dipping constellations and then looked down to the expanse of the village below them. It had the appearance of a drab phantom. They could barely see people's dwelling houses set below them haphazardly and sandwiched between jagged stones and boulders. Some were lit with dim lights. Their rooftops were grass thatched and mud smeared walls. None of them had the semblance of permanence, except for the Oldman's house. Whenever torrential rains came, some of the homes would be washed away in the tide towards Buhani River, all the way to the Lake. Gusting wind swept through them as well as over them. Between the roof and the wall, a larger gaping space remained, making it ideal for ventilation. It is no wonder people in this village never died of carbon monoxide poisoning emitted from their koroboi lamps.

Fumes of smoke from burning wood drifted all the way to the summit of the hill mingled with sweet smells of different kinds of foods: fish, chicken, beef, burning *ugali*; they smelt it all. They were certain some lazy women were still cooking their supper. Distantly, they could hear murmured gossip and sporadic laughter piercing the night. They could also hear sounds of flapping wings as bats stole out of the cave and vanished into darkness.

No sooner had the sounds of fluttering wings died down, than Kahuga's past decadent life reversed into his present . . .

"Agoyi," Kahugasaid casually.

"What?" Agoyi said as though he were irritated by the sound of Kahuga's voice.

"Did I ever tell you about the time Keya flogged me until my buttocks were as swollen as plumb cassavas?"

"No!" Agoyi said nonchalantly.

"It was one sunny Monday morning," Kahuga said. "I did something so stupid."

"Something tells me I can't picture this one," Agoyi remarked.

"Keya's goat had just delivered its ewe; it was brown with a touch of white around the sides of its hind legs. Uuh! It was the most beautiful ewe I had ever seen. During its first six days of life, I would steal into its stall and just look at it. Occasionally, it roamed outside, but always within its mother's range."

"On the day Keya bludgeoned me, I do not know what possessed me. I walked into that stall with a brown manila bag in my hand . . . I was drunk stupid with mischief and excitement. Adrenaline rushed through me like a bad poison. When I stepped inside the stall, the putrid smell of heavy goat urine ambushed me. On the floor, tiny round pellets of goat faeces were scattered everywhere. The ewe was suckling and nudging at its mother's udders, hitting it from time to time with its head. It was as though, in so doing, milk would gash into its mouth. Creamy-like slime from its sides oozed out, foaming at the mouth. When it saw me, the goat bleated. The ewe stopped suckling, staring at me with its bright eyes. My nose began to twitch, and I dared not scratch. I just wanted to get my hands on that furry creature.

Although it was beautiful, I was not attracted to it for its beauty; I was drawn to it simply for the pounds it could fetch me.

Without thinking, I advanced slowly towards the ewe. It ran to the opposite side of its mother. Its mother bleated again. I was in no hurry to alert Desi of what I was doing, for she was the only one at home at the time. I kept a low profile for a moment and then dove for the ewe. It hopped up in effort to avoid me, but I grabbed one of its hind legs and held onto it tightly, but careful enough not to injure it. I pulled it towards me, captured it, and stuffed it into my manila bag. Immediately, I bolted out of the stall with the bag firmly and securely tucked under my armpit. I raced out of the compound as quickly as I could. I knew where I had to go: Luanda Market. After all, it was market day, and I knew it would not be difficult for me to get rid of the little goat. As I ran, the ewe bleated and kicked me wanting to free itself. The more it kicked me, the harder I pressed against the rim of my bag, shutting it tightly in there.

As I made my way from home along the narrow footpath heading down the murram road, I realized, as though for the first time, the terrain was rough. The path was steep and ruggedly treacherous, not to mention the weight of the ewe weighted me down. As I scuttled on, I kept on banging my bare feet on stones, sandy pebbles, prickly thorns, and on anything and everything. I ducked regularly to avoid injuring my eyes as leaves from shrubs whacked me on my face, hampering my vision. The wind crushed violently against my forehead as I scampered on, causing my eyes to water. I wiped my tears off with my free hand while the other tightly held onto the bag. Blazing sun caused my body to drip in sweat, but I continued running. The ewe, intermittently, hit me in my rib cage. I felt excruciating pain, but the thought of pounds . . . Twenty pounds, thirty pounds, forty pounds, seemed worth all the pain.

I ran and ran and ran, as fast as I could, much like a cheetah, not even bothering to greet those whom I encountered along the way; this was bad. Some frowned at my impudent behaviour while others simply moved out of my way. The pipers threatened to report me to Keya, but I did not care.

When I came down the marrum road, I followed the narrow footpath past the Oldman's home toward the Msheba River. In my haste, I narrowly forced an elderly woman off the road. I did not pay her any attention. I just raced on. Distantly, I heard her mumbling something like: "I wonder what is wrong with that boy! Always running and running." I did not hear anything else she said.

The footpath veered slightly to the north and then turned sharply west bound, snaking towards the river. I still had to fight shrubbery and prickly thorns. That did not stop me. I ran as though oblivious to the world around me. Unfortunately, a sharp thorn pierced one of the soles of my feet, which was as hard as the Ngoroke stones. It was a mystery to me as to how it had succeeded in burying itself in my sole. Seething pain crept up my body. I bent down and blinked hard at the spot. I took a lick of my finger and gently rubbed against the sore; again, maddening pain crawled to every inch of my body. The ewe which I still carried in my bag and under my armpit gave me a good kicking. "Rats!" I squirmed painfully. I hated it.

Realizing I still had a long way to go to Luanda, I stood up and hopped on my good foot for a second. Then, I pushed my bad foot onto the ground. Oh! I experienced such excruciating pain. I ground my teeth trying to block the pain off my mind. The goat bleated obliterating any discomfort I felt. The end was more enticing than a mere thorn buried in my foot. At that juncture, I was blind to rational thought and inured to my physical pain; I consoled myself that physical pain was only, but temporal and would soon pass.

In my haste to press forward, my good foot got entangled in a protruding and meandering root-like-vine. I flew up in the air, landing on the ground face down. The force with which my body slammed onto the hard surface caused my head to churn like swirling eddies. I nearly lost my consciousness, but the bleating sound of the ewe: "Mee! Mee! Mee!" reeled me back to my senses. An elderly woman who was coming from the direction of the river saw me and dashed towards me, worried that I may have injured myself or crushed my skull. As she drew closer to me, she was dismayed to hear the sound of the braying ewe.

"What in the world are you doing with that?" she said her eyes popping wide open. As soon as she realized what it was I held captive in my bag, she lifted her handbag up high and smacked me hard on my head, which was already swirling with intense hurt. Sensing my danger, I did not stay long to respond. I scooped myself off the ground, pushing her out of my way. And like lightening, I hurried on, cool air brushing gently against my forehead.

Poor woman . . . had she known, she would have minded her own business. Distantly, I heard her body flop into the nearby bush . . . I did not look back to see or listen. Vaguely, I heard her screaming and cursing me for my loutishness. Instantaneously, panic jolted me as I realized that running with a goat in a manila bag all the way to Luanda was sheer idiocy; not only that, but a week old ewe was purely insane. Whatever possessed me, I do not know.

As I drew close to the river, I heard her screaming: '*Wolololo*! *Umwiivi*! *Umwiivi*—Thief! Thief!' She was screaming at the top of her lungs. Right away I knew what that meant. I ducked into the bush. Across the river, I heard a male voice bawl: '*Haai*--where?'

"He is coming over there!" she yelled back.

"Suddenly, I heard sounds of footsteps from almost every direction heading towards where the woman was. I lay low, hoping that the ewe would remain still; I was wrong. Almost immediately, it bleated. My heart began to pound hard against my rib cage. I contemplated releasing it, but it was too late."

"Find that boy!" I heard the woman say as loud as she could. Boys. Men. Women. Young and old all emerged from their homes to catch the thief. Immediately, I began to feel like a caged animal, much like the ewe I had imprisoned in my manila bag.

Meanwhile, Keya had returned home to an empty stall. He could not believe his ewe was missing. He still had the use of his eyes then—he later lost his sight to glaucoma. He looked everywhere, but could not see it. He was certain it could not have wandered off by itself; after all, it was only six days old. Anxiety stirred in him profusely, forcing him to scram out of his compound hunting for his missing ewe.

He, like Kahuga, took the narrow footpath to the marrum road, fighting with the treacherous thorns, sandy pebbles, and stones. His eyes gawked everywhere, while his ears were attuned to all sounds around him: from the mooing of cows, the bleating of sheep and goats, the clucking of hens, to the children's running sent by their parents to the *duka* to make a quick purchase. Unlike them, Keya was running for a different reason: he had to find his ewe. As he emerged on the marrum road, he heard people talking about the young lad with a goat in a bag. One woman, in particular was saying, "Truly I tell you! I saw him with my own eyes. Uuh! He just ran into me like a bulldozer. He nearly knocked me over. He is wearing a red cap and a brown jacket . . . he was heading towards the river. Kids these days have no manners. He also had this big manila bag tucked under . . .

Hearing this, Keya did not waste time waiting for the woman to finish her story. He knew it had to be Kahuga because he was the only young man in the entire Ngoroke village who liked to wear a red cap. He understood the implication of what Kahuga had done. He also knew if he did not get to him in time, he would end up with a funeral before dusk. If only the boy had not lost his parents to AIDS two years ago, he would have expelled him from his home.

Closing his mind to the woman's voice, he started running as fast as he could and running he did. Beads of sweat formed on his forehead, but he ran on. In a mad fury, his eyes gaped wide as he marched on, looking for his grandson. As he raced beyond the Oldman's home, people in most homesteads had already begun to emerge onto the path, alerted to the commotion. They, too, had been startled by the woman's heckling.

Keya nearly knocked the very woman Kahuga had shoved into the shrub off the path as he made the sharp turn towards the river.

"Did you see him?" he asked the woman as he raced on.

"Who?"

"The boy with the goat."

"See him?"she said furiously. "He nearly killed me!"

"Yes, him. Where did he go?'

"He went that way," she said pointing a finger in the direction of the river.

No sooner had she finished than Keya took off in a flash. He had to get to the boy before anyone else did. 'They'll surely kill him,' he thought. Logooli people had a strong dislike of thieves. They had no respect for them whatsoever and exercised mob justice any time they caught one, always! Better a dead thief than a live one.

Swarms of men and women were now on the mission to find the thief. Some of the men carried with them their *rungus* ready to make good use of them. Keya did not want his grandson to face the wrath of the mob.

"I heard his footsteps as he ran towards the river."

"'Have you seen my boy?'" I heard Keya say as he drew close to where I was.

"Your boy, your boy?" someone queried. "You mean the thief is your boy?"

"No, my grandson is not a thief," he lied. He hoped such lie would save him. It did.

Luck was not on my side that day. The stupid ewe bleated, giving me away.

I emerged out of hiding on my own volition in shame to the flustered eyes of my grandfather. He was angry, ashamed, and embarrassed. No doubt, I knew I was going to receive a sound whipping. Better that than the wrath of the neighbours: a burning tire around my neck. Keya dragged me all the way home. He did not say much on the way, but I knew he was very angry. I could tell because he kept on grinding his teeth and inflating the veins of his neck like a monitor lizard.

No sooner had we arrived home than he retreated into the house only to emerge later with his leather belt. I could not run away because I knew I was as guilty as hell. I accepted my punishment like a man.

"Whatever possessed you to steal the goat," Keya said as his leather whip crushed hard on my bottom.

I squealed in pain, grinding my teeth, but not daring to shed a tear out of pride. The whip flew up in the air and crash landed on my bottom again and again and again. When it was all over, I had innumerable swellings on my buttocks the size of a plump cassava," Kahuga said laughing, his voice dying to the chirping sounds of crickets.

"That was some story!" Agoyi said.

"What do you suppose might happen to us if we failed?"

"We can't fail," Kahuga said cockily. "We can't fail." Then he withdrew into silence.

The dead of night crept over them as they sat, awaiting the appearance of Chonjo, the Dispatcher. Murmured gossip and sporadic laughter continued to pierce the night. Frogs croaked. Crickets chirped. Bats flapped their wings and time marched on . . .

Although the night was dark and heavily overcast, the boys could still count how many homes had their lights on for a very long period of time. They contemplated how they could sneak into some of the homes by simply stealing their way through the gaping opening between the wall and the roof. What a dangerous thought, definitely not ideal in a situation, which warranted an expeditious exit. They needed an in and out kind of job. Nothing more, nothing less. Quick and simple. Homes that had dogs were out of question.

"If we entered a home with a dog," Kahuga speculated. "We would have to have a bone or some meat!"

"How would that help us?" Agoyi asked.

"We would have to trap the dog with it."

"You are a crafty dog!" Agoyi exclaimed.

"While it's nibbling on it, you and I could go in."

"That is absolutely clever! But what if . . ."

"Hold on! I have an even better idea," Kahuga added. "If we have enough money from our transaction, we could buy a quarter kilo of steak, get an old battery and then grid that thin film in its centre. We could hide it inside the meat and give it to the dog; that way, we might not have a problem with it."

"But that would kill it," Agoyi protested.

"Precisely my point!" Kahuga said affirmatively.

"You are a devil . . . a real devil walking on twos! I can't do that," Agoyi said bitterly. Killing is bad. It is a moral sin even if it is a dog. He even threatened to leave the group, but this was an empty threat. "No! No killing of animals. No killing of people . . . understood? Or else, I am out!"

Kahuga stiffened mumbling, "Okay *bwana*, you don't have to get all rattled over a mere dog! Can't you take a joke?"

"That was a very bad joke!"

Just as the stars seemed to sink deeper into the dipping constellation in the darkened sky and the boys were consumed by its majestic nature, Chonjo, the Dispatcher, a roguish-looking boy, not much older than Agoyi, skulked on the boys like a witch. His feet were light, muffled by the sounds of crackling guava leaves. Agoyi jumped out of fright. He had this hair-raising experience; his body shuddered. Kahuga, too, jumped out of fright.

"Are you out of your mind?" Kahuga said in a tone that registered both fear and joy after realizing who it was.

"Am sorry," Chonjo said in a feigned pretence to be serious. Both Kahuga and Agoyi knew he was not sorry.

"What took you so long?" Kahuga said surly.

"I am here, am I not?" Chonjo remarked snobbishly. Agoyi hissed with displeasure.

"Okay, here is the deal!" Kahuga said.

"This guy here," he said pointing a finger at Agoyi. "His name is Agoyi and has custody of our merchandise."

"You mean him? Isn't he the one we . . ." he said flicking the switch on his sport-light and flashing Agoyi's face.

"Of course . . . In deed he is!" Kahuga cut him short, not wanting him to mention the incident.

Chonjo scrutinized Agoyi intensely from head-to-toe like a meat inspector. He walked around him, front to back and front. "You trust him?"

"Of course. Absolutely. No doubt!" Kahuga said. "Do you have a problem with that?"

"No. Not really! . . . just making sure."

"Agoyi has our goods from our last job."

"I see!"

"Can you dispose it off tomorrow?"

"No problem, I'll see what I can do!" the Dispatcher affirmed.

"Then it's concluded," Kahuga said. "You'll pick the grains from Agoyi's home tonight."

"No problem . . . brother!"

After that, the boys remained on the summit for a very long time. Time did not seem to move at a steady pace . . . it dragged on and on, but they did not seem to care. They plotted their next heist, which they wanted to tackle right away . . .

Chapter 20

That night, the boys talked, talked, and talked for hours, and though their conversation was marred by disagreements, they occasionally fused as one under a hearty laughter over an idyllic reminiscence of their prior pranks. Then their conversation turned to their impending heist, a jagged mountain they had to climb. The success on this mission would forever be remembered in the village after many years to come, and they were right.

Occasionally, Kahuga appealed to the other boys:

"People this heist is a test of my manhood, *our* manhood . . . Agoyi are you in?"

"Let me think!" Agoyi said.

"No man! The time for thinking is over. It is time for action," Chonjo, the Dispatcher chimed in.

"Yes! It is time for action," kahuga affirmed. "Fear is out of the question."

Agoyi was not convinced. He still had fear of capture. Fear of imprisonment. Yes! He had to overcome these fears. No matter what, he had to . . . And that was a fact. A cool wind passed. Then silence fell between them. There was no sound. There was no sound near them, not even from the village below. The village had the appearance of a sleeping giant. No sign of life. The murmur in people's houses had died down. The laughter, too, had died down. The whiff of smoke and the aroma of good food, even it, too, was no more; only the sounds of chirping crickets filled the air. Fire flies glided into the open, flickering their lights on and off in the darkened night. No night-runner anywhere. Just silence, as though there was nothing left in this grand universe, but the glitter of stars streaming, ceaselessly through the black stillness of the night.

When the boys finally decided to return home, they descended the slope in silence. Their knees wobbled with each step they took. The terrain down was treacherous, a truth to which they were accustomed. Terry shrubs were everywhere, which they pushed aside with their hands to pave the way. Sharp pebbles and prickly thorns that occasionally pierced the soles of their feet were routine. They were in no hurry to get there, but time continued to march on at a steady pace.

As they continued their slow descent to the village, they stopped at the slightest noise of popping twigs only to realize it was nothing . . . just a crackling shrub.

The boys made a quick stop at Kahuga's home. They picked-up some tools: a crow bar, a *rungu* and left. They walked in a single file, at a steady pace, and in absolute silence. Kahuga led the way, Chonjo, the Dispatcher and Agoyi followed . . .

The three boys arrived at their next victim's gate around midnight. They stopped abruptly to listen. The house was a large stucco home with steel doors and windows, giving it a facade of a maximum-security prison. Inside, it appeared dark because the lights were out. This indicated that its occupants were already asleep. Everything was soundless. The air around them was cool and crispy. Up and above, the sky was pitch black.

"What a peaceful night!" Agoyi noted as though enticed by the irresistible freedom of the open horizon dotted by a constellation of stars—flowing to the east beyond Maragoli Hills that harbours light and darkness, and to the west, way beyond Mung'oma Caves.

"Very much so," Kahuga said.

Filled with a fear of being caught, the boys stealthily stole into the compound through a barbed-wire fence in a prowler like manner, exercising caution. They crept to the front door, peered through its tiny cracks to see if the occupants were still awake, but there was no indication of life. Gently, Kahuga twisted the knob, but the door was bolted from inside. They tip-toed to the back, but the sight of the tightly welded door made Kahuga's jaws drop with disappointment. Agoyi pushed his ear to the hard cold door to listen, but everything inside was soundless, save for the chirping sounds of crickets and croaking of frogs near the water tank. There were no cracks in the door. Common sense told them the inside was just as dark as the outside; and if not, even much darker than the outside.

Because both the back door and window were made of steel, it was a daunting task, impossibility for the boys. The doors were professionally welded by a skilled *jua kali* that no crow-bar could tamper with its lock. Kahuga could picture the man's eyes behind his safety eyeglasses as he ogled into the blue flames of his welding machine as he fused the steel into a perfect solid door or window, almost burglar-proof. Fiery sparks flew into air as the flames came in contact with the metal.

The boys crawled to the back window of the house which opened into the granary. As expected, it was bolted from inside. This was not going to be an easy ordeal, not a wooden latch like was the case at Keya's house. So they stood there, by the window, thinking . . . And thinking they did. Then, a bad thought crept on Agoyi's mind:

"Kahuga," he whispered. "What if a night-runner is hiding in there?"

"Where?"

"Underneath the tree?"

"That won't happen!"

"How can you be so sure?"

"Trust me . . . I know!"

"But how?"

"Night runners are afraid of people."

"Are you sure?"

"Really!"

"I don't trust you!"

"Nothing is going to happen to us."

"Okay! Let us hope so."

Turning around the corner, towards the kitchen, the boys took a few more steps, stopping at the water tank. A few yards, south of the tank, was a thick vivacious banana plantation and smacked right in its centre was a tall colossus avocado tree. Its towering branches were massive and stooped slightly, weighted by avocado fruits, which were as huge as papayas, an ideal place to hide in case they were pursued. Underneath the tree and protruding from the soil around its giant trunk, bulging roots separated the soil, leaving behind enormous cracks enough to swallow an entire goat. The soil around it was unproductive for any other crop to grow. The area was bare and as dry as a desert . . . No grass, no life, nothing.

That night, the boys conceded defeat, but not before Kahuga devised a new plan, an even more insidious plot. It was one he knew would work in their favour as long as they exercised caution . . .

"What shall we do now?" Agoyi asked his companion who was the brain of the entire operation.

"I am still thinking!" he paused. "Follow me," he said after a while.

Without uttering a word, both Agoyi and Chonjo, the Dispatcher trudged behind. The boys tip-toed to the south end of the house. There was an enormous water tank a couple of feet away from the wall of the main house. It faced the avocado tree.

The boys sat on the slab by the tank as Kahuga paced around it. He inspected it—up and down and around it. He sat down again. He moved his right hand to his chin in a contemplative pose, his mind racing . . . conjuring up wild thoughts, an improbable problem.

"I got it! I got it!"

"What?"

"Let us go in through the roof!" he said after giving the idea a significant thought.

"Are you out of your mind?" Agoyi said perplexed.

"You heard me! Let us go in through the roof."

"How do you plan to do that?" Chonjo asked in puzzlement.

"Simple! I will show you."

"You are out of your mind! You are crazy . . . that is what you are. A crazy bastard, a lunatic!" Agoyi protested. "That is what you are . . . a crazy lunatic!"

Inwardly, Agoyi wondered: 'How can we pry open the roof of the house without drawing attention to ourselves? It can't be done. That is it. It can't be done. Period!' Unfortunately, or fortunately, the word impossible was completely out of Kahuga's vocabulary. He would not hear of it. Once deciding on anything, he executed it without question.

"No! I am not crazy. My plan is swift. You will see."

"Listen!" Kahuga said. "This is what we shall do . . ."

Kahuga explained to them his plan. It was very simple. The boys would crawl along the wall of the water tank like spiders. Once on the top of the tank, they would hop onto the roof and using a crow bar, pry it open. They would then lift the corrugated zinc sheets off and jump into the granary. It was that simple. They would open the window and use it as an outlet to sweep the storage clean. Ultimately, they have to exit the house the same way, replacing the roof afterwards to conceal their crime.

With the plan now imprinted upon their minds, the boys embarked on their first attempt. As usual, Kahuga took the lead. Like a prowler, which, indeed, he was; he began his ascent of the tank. Agoyi turned the spotlight on and off, casting a temporary glow on the wall and allowing his friend to see where he was going. Kahuga's first attempt was a sad flop. He had not even climbed halfway when his foot slipped from under him. He landed on the hard cemented area around the tank. He squealed, shifting his position with a small cry, as of a soft pain or agony. The other two boys giggled.

"Hush," Kahuga warned. "You will awaken the house."

The boys fell silent.

Kahuga did not move. He just sat there absorbing the shock of his pain. Though he did not want to admit it, he, inwardly, questioned the success of his plan. Nevertheless, being the optimist he was, he did not dwell much on the impossibilities of their mission; he brushed these thoughts off his mind without delay. A cool draft passed, gently brushing against his exposed skin. The thick banana leaves rustled. The leaves of the avocado tree whooshed. The surge of the wind died to the sound of something big crinkling the banana leaves and then dropping onto the ground with a loud bang. Startled, Agoyi jumped, sticking onto Kahuga like a tick on a cow. The boys stuck to each other, as though glued together and never to separate. Nerves made the muscles of their stomachs tighten. Kahuga's heart thumped rapidly. Agoyi's heart pounded fast. The Dispatcher's raced.

"Shh!" Agoyi said. "There has to be a night-runner around!"

"Control yourself, will you?" Kahuga barked.

"What if he is there? What if he can recognize us?" Agoyi complained.

"Hush you fool!" the Dispatcher said sternly, pretending to be brave.

Unbeknownst to the boys, a night-runner is always frightened of being caught. Rumour has it that whenever a male night-runner goes out, his wife must stay awake until his safe return home, with one of her feet propped on one of the stones of her three-dimensional stove tending to the fire, which must not be extinguished. A slip of the foot off the stone signalled bad luck.

"No, there is no night-runner!"Kahuga said finally.

The boys were still huddled together, and their backs pressed hard onto the cold concrete tank. Another draft passed and more rustling leaves continued to unnerve the boys, closely following with the sound of things falling down. It was only then the boys realized what had startled them was no night-runner, but avocadoes whose weight overpowered the tinny twig upon which they hung.

"Those damned avocadoes nearly gave me a heart attack," Agoyi complained as he loosened his firm grip off his friend.

That night, the boys aborted their operation promising to complete it the next night . . .

Chapter 21

The next day was Friday. The dawn opened to a thunderous roar. People could barely hear the sounds of roosters crowing to introduce the day break; for their cawing was muffled by the heavy pounding of rain above the rooftops of their houses. Even Irene, Ngoroke's daily dawn caller, remained safe in her house. No brave soul dared to go out in such down pour. It was as though the bowels of the heavenly dikes had opened their floodgates upon earth. Intermittent lightening flashed across the horizon accompanied with deafening roars. The hills were grey and misty, and the sky remained heavily overcast and saturated for the entire day. On the horizon, there was no orange effulgence, just dark clouds gliding slowly like a ball of fluffy cotton.

That evening the boys did not meet on the summit as they regularly did; instead, Kahuga snuck into Agoyi's house. There the boys sat, listening to the deafening synchronized sounds of rain as it crashed hard on the corrugated rooftop. Strong winds swayed trees outside. Destruction accompanied it. Boulders bolted from their base, rolling down slopes like torpedoes. Weak trees and branches fell victim to gusting wind, breaking off without warning. Brown water flowed everywhere, forming uncountable streams towards the Buhani River. Valiant souls, men and women, young and old, occasionally and briskly braved the rain, venturing outside to find food.

Outside, the Oldman's chickens stood in the veranda seeking shelter from the rain. They appeared cold. Their heads drooped, while their feathers damp with rain, sagged on the sides of their bodies. Chicks hid safely in their mother's wings; only their pointy beaks, thief-like, peeked through the sodden feathers. As for the boys, they sat in silence listening to music and contemplating their next plan.

Occasionally, they swapped stories. It was during that time that Kahuga remembered an incident which had happened in their village not long ago . . .

"Agoyi," Kahuga began as he always did whenever he wanted to fib; though the story he was about to tell was no fib. It had happened and most Ngorokeans have yet to come to grips with it.

"Did I ever tell you about Sambaya?"

"No! Who is he?"

"Oh that Sambaya was a very strange character!"

"What was strange about him?"

"Let me tell you . . . he was one uncanny man . . . he was more of a social recluse. He lived alone and never married. He never did anything to harm others, but it is what we did to him."

"You and whom?"

"Chonjo and me . . . we go way back then!"

"Exactly what did you do to him, kill him?"

"No, but what we did to him was not right."

For just a fraction of a second, Agoyi wondered if Kahuga had a conscience, enabling him to distinguish right from wrong. "And what was that?" he asked.

"Well, Sambaya was a poor farmer whose house was located not very far from Mung'oma Caves. His land extended all the way to the stream to the base of the caverns. The land was very fertile, and he could have planted a lot of vegetables, but he never did. Instead, he had a big plantation of sugarcane and yams. He hardly planted maize or vegetables. He only had patience with his sugarcane. He tended to it day in and day out and kept a vigilant watch of it. When it matured, he chopped it, and hauled it to the market for a quick sell."

"One time Chonjo and I conned him out of his sugarcane and he didn't even know it. He was such a dimwit . . . Yup! He was a dimwit, alright. We even coined a name for him . . . the "*odinglous man*," our nonsensical term for an idiot.

"You sly dog!" Agoyi said.

"What we did was stupid. I only had five shillings in my pocket when we walked up to him. I pretended I wanted to buy a portion of his cane. I pulled out one from the pile. It was succulent. I started to haggle with him."

"How many notches for five shillings," I asked him.

"Six," he said.

"Old man you want to rob me?"

"You know the amount!" he protested.

"You are too expensive," I said.

"If you don't want to buy it, go away," he said, pushing me out of the way.

While I distracted him, the Dispatcher pulled out one cane, vanishing behind the shops. I watched him until he was out of view. Sambaya and I could not strike a deal, which was my intent. I walked off empty handed to his cursing."

"I walked around the corner where I met Chonjo."

"You rogue! . . . You dirty thieving rogue! You started your mischiefa long time ago!"

"No, but let us just say . . ."

"You didn't have anything to do with his death . . . Did you?"

"No!"

"You stole his sugarcane forcing him to die of hunger."

"No, but he died of starvation alright!"

"You killed the man . . . that is just it! You killed the man."

"No, he died of starvation," Kahuga said again.

"How do you know that?"

"Someone found him dead. He was alone. His body had signs of decomposition, which meant he must have been dead for days before people realized he was missing."

"Didn't he have a wife?"

"No!"

"How about children?"

"His loins were not blessed that way."

"His death had nothing to do with his sugarcane?"

"No. The sugarcane incident happened a few years ago. When he died, he was old and frail."

"So how did he die?" Agoyi asked again as though he was not convinced by Kahuga's explanation.

"He starved to death," Kahuga said again.

"You have already said that . . . give me some details will you!"

"The man who found him said when Sambaya died he was busy scraping *amaloondo*—burnt bits of corn meal—from his cooking pot!" Kahuga said breaking into a heart-felt laughter.

"How did he know that?"

"Because he had found the dead man's left hand tightly clenched on the rim of his pot. He had cleaned the entire pot with the nails of his right hand, the residue of which was wedged in his nails," Kahuga added, still laughing and cupping his hand to demonstrate how the man's hand had clamped onto the pot.

"That is sad," Agoyi said as silence fell upon them.

Heavy rains continued to pound on the rooftop above them as the growl of thunder passed. In their muteness,

Agoyi wondered what his grandmother would say if she knew he burglarized a blind man and his deaf wife. Not only that even his father would be disappointed. Common sense told him he should get out of the gang before it was too late, but he was already too deep in it to bail-out. Perhaps, it was the thrill of doing the impossible that overpowered his rational thoughts. Or, perhaps, it was the fear of being lashed that overcame his good judgement. A flashing light appeared over the wall accompanied by thunder, but the boys sat sullenly reposed for a very long time.

After the rains had subsided, Kahuga suggested they proceed with the heist as planned.

"I think we should still do it tonight!"

"Just the two of us?"

"Why not?"

"We can't manage this job. Besides, the others are not here."

"Nonsense. I think we should try it."

"No!"

"Where is your adventure?"

"Are you out of your mind?" Agoyi said.

"Do I look like someone out of his mind?" Kahuga said irritated

"I don't think the two of us can do it. Only a lunatic can contemplate doing *it* during or after the rain."

"I think this is a perfect time," Kahuga added affirmatively.

"Why is that so?"

"No one can hear us. With the rains pounding on the rooftop, those inside might not distinguish between rain and us prying the nails off the roof."

Agoyi pressed his back much deeper into his chair and remained sullenly still as though divorced from his present. His eyes vacantly stared outside, glossing over the rain as it fell relentlessly over an already saturated earth.

Kahuga did not pester him about it. Instead, he developed a posture of ultimate contemplation. He rested his chin between the palms of his hands and gazed on the ground. Time seemed stagnant, save for the rain that continued its relentless pounding of the rooftop.

"Are you in or out?" Kahuga asked Agoyi in a sharp unyielding tone. He did not lift his head to look at him.

Agoyi's body stiffened. He shifted his gaze from outside to Kahuga whose head was still fixated to the ground. He repositioned his weight on the chair, and it creaked. Kahuga moved his eyes slowly and gawked at him; their unyielding eyes met. There was silence.

"I want out!" Agoyi announced a little bit later.

"What?"

"You heard me! I want out!"

"You can't be serious." Kahuga said as he sat bolt-upright and giving Agoyi an angry look. "You can't do that now!" There was a fire in his eyes.

"I just did."

"What has become of you?"

"I can't do it. These are my folks. I couldn't live with myself . . . besides, it is morally wrong."

"Do that and you are dead! Do you hear me? You are dead. You didn't think of that when we broke into my folks' home did you?"

"You didn't tell me they were your folks."

"It doesn't matter! You made a commitment to the gang."

"I just can't do it!"

"If you don't . . . well, don't blame me. I could turn you into the law too. All I have to say is you were the one who broke into my folk's home. You'll go to jail for it. Who will believe you? Am sure you are no saint!"

Nervous, Agoyi broke into a cold sweat. He was afraid of the law. He was afraid of his folks. What would he tell them?

"Mark my words, I will turn you in!"

There was silence between them as the rains continued to fall at a steady pace.

Out of fear, he begrudgingly mumbled: "Okay!"

"Okay what?"

"I am in!"

Kahuga broke in a heckling laughter, "You had me fooled for a minute ago."

Agoyi grinned nervously. "Let us go before I change my mind."

"You won't regret this!" Kahuga said, but he was wrong. Agoyi was already regretful of his decision

As the boys walked out of the house, it was a little past eleven at night. The sky was still overcast, and the ground was inundated. Drizzles of rain continued to fall steadily. Everywhere they stepped was wet, but that did not matter. They had to execute the plan, no matter inclement weather.

They made their way to the victim's water tank in a matter of minutes. They were soaking wet. A quick and thorough inspection of the compound followed. Everything was quiet except for a slight glow of light inside the house, and that could pause a problem.

Without wasting time, a drenched Kahuga began to climb up the tank. It was slippery and he slipped off, landing on the hard cemented surface. He felt a sharp pain crawl all over his body. He shook it off vigorously, but to no avail. He made a second, third, and fourth attempt, but he slipped off again, each time.

"Agoyi," he whispered "Give me a push will you?"

"Why didn't you say so in the first place?"

Agoyi locked his fingers together, cupped his palms, sprawled his feet to have a solid footing and then asked Kahuga to take a climb. He thrust his left foot in Agoyi's palms. With one powerful heave, he propelled Kahuga's body forward. Kahuga flung his hands to the edge of the tank and held onto it firmly. With his feet dangling mid-air, Agoyi repositioned, stretched his hands-up, pushed him once more and until he pounced on top of the tank. He stood still, listening for any stir within the house. There was no one, just silence. He sighed joyously . . . The first hurdle was over.

"Pass me the light!" Kahuga commanded.

Agoyi fished for the light from his jacket. "Here!" he said stretching to hand it to him. Kahuga bent on his knees to grasp it.

"It's your turn now!"

"I can't come-up there!"

"Come-on, I'll assist you."

"No!"

"Hurry-up! This is not a time to argue about this."

A reluctant Agoyi, with Kahuga's assistance mounted the tank. Although it was cold and wet, the boys hardly felt it. Their minds were engrossed with the heist so much so that it numbed their physical chilliness.

Drenched to the skin, the boys embarked on their task promptly. Diligently, and meticulously, they worked. Most people would have dared not work in the rain, out of fear of contracting Malaria. The chilling symptoms of Malaria, shivering or gagging, would have been enough to bar one from going into the rain. The boys pried the nails off the corrugated zinc sheets with their crow bar, one nail at a time, but careful enough not to rouse suspicion of those inside. After each successful extraction, they stopped to observe their progress or to listen. Hearing nothing, they moved onto the next nail prying it off gently. Agoyi flashed, and Kahuga pried the nails off. Each time, the slanting beams of the spotlight touched the iron sheets, throwing an almost slender, but distorted shadow of Kahuga upon the streaked glitter of rain upon the roof. When he had successfully loosened one sheet, he lifted it off the roof and flashed inside the granary. A sea of sacks of grain filled the room. Kahuga's eyes, lacerated with greed, bulged with excitement. "Holy mother of God!" he gasped. "What have we here? Marvellous, absolutely marvellous!"

Right away, Kahuga aborted the robbery that night. Instead, he promised to return the next night. The lust in his heart was so great that taking half of the loot was out of the question. He had to have it all.

To return the zinc sheet back in place, the boys worked quietly for an interval of fifteen minutes, but leaving the nail loose enough for when they returned. When they finished, they descended the roof and walked back to Agoyi's hut dripping wet like two water carts. They were hungry and cold, but there was no food to quiet their hunger or tea to warm their chilled bodies. Kahuga paced the floor while Agoyi withdrew to his bedroom, changed, and returned to Kahuga's pacing.

When Kahuga left Agoyi's house that night, it was still raining. He pushed his red cap tightly on his head, zipped his jacket, and walked into the rain. Agoyi followed him with his eyes until his shape was nothing more than a tiny speck. He pulled the door shut behind him to the growling of thunder, but he could still hear the rain beat softly upon the shingles. . .

After Kahuga had left, Agoyi retreated to his bedroom. He dropped his tired and cold body onto his bed, face up. His mind was disturbed with what had just transpired. He drew both his hands up and crossed them upon his chest; he had the semblance of a dead man and, probably, he was a dead man. Inwardly, he wanted to pray, asking God for forgiveness, but he could not. There was no prayer throughout the world that could save his damned soul. So he lay there in still repose, gazing at the ceiling.

His mind replayed intrinsic details of his past decadent life: From his arrival at his grandfather's home, Desi and Keya's robbery, to their impending heist. The image of Kahuga prying the nails on the roof remained and continued to seethe on his psyche . . . His drenched clothes stuck to his body as though glued to it, and warm mucus seeping out of his nose like honey from a bottle. He imagined what the Oldman would say if he caught them. How about his father? How about his grandmother? He had no answer for these questions.

He reached out for his koroboi lamp, turned it off and closed his eyes save for his thoughts. Soon, he started to doze off, zooming in and out of his pulsing present. He had not been completely wrapped under the tender hands of slumber when a dazzling image of a woman appeared to him in a sparkling white sheer dress. She was an angelic spectre. Her image morphed into that of his mother, and she was beckoning him to join her. Her vision drew warm tears to his eyes. Seeing her, he started to weep. Warm tears glided down his face. Without thinking, he sprang on his feet and opened his arms wide wanting to embrace her. The closer he drew to her, the further she retreated. He did not care; his angelic mother was within reach. On her dimpled face, a soft smile hung loosely, melting Agoyi's troubled spirit.

She continued to beckon him with her hand delicately draped with an exquisite white sheer shawl.

"Mama," Agoyi yelled, but no words come out. "Mama!" he said again, his eyes sparkling behind their eyelids. "Am I glad to see you . . . Finally!" The female form simply stared at him. She was still smiling, and luring him towards her. Her feet floated gracefully above him. Agoyi followed her with his eyes as though held by her hypnotic smile or an invisible chain. He lifted his right hand wanting to touch her, just the tips of her fingers, but she whirled away, vanishing into oblivion. Agoyi emerged from his stupor with his lips pursed mumbling, "Mother! Mother! Please don't go!" However, she was gone . . .

Chapter 22

Daybreak came sooner than Agoyi had anticipated. He woke to the first ray of light penetrating into his bedroom through the cracks in his window. His eyes were still heavy with sleep, but he could not continue to linger in bed. Slothfulness was not one of his character traits. He hopped out of bed and stretched his body. He stretched some more before walking out of the house. The air was pitilessly raw and cold. He buttoned his shirt to keep warm. As he stepped outside, the ground was moist, the sky a clear blue, and the sun so bright that his vision was blurred. He rubbed and squint his eyes several times struggling to see. When his sight cleared, his eyes wandered slowly eastwards beyond Maragoli Hills into the furthest horizons. The Hills were misty though, through it, the sun peeped, radiating a beautiful orange glow.

When his eyes became accustomed to the light, he headed to the cowshed to begin his morning chore: milk the cows. The cowshed was wet and muddy with cow dung. Pungent smell of dung ambushed him as he straddled inside. It took him awhile to ready himself for the task at hand. He hauled dung out of the way before milking the cows.

When he was done, he walked to his grandmother's kitchen to get warm water and a milking jug. His grandmother was sitting on a stool tending to the fire. Its wood was softly lit. The interior of the thick-walled little kitchen was dimly lit, and his grandmother had deliberately not lit her kerosene lamp. Without a word to him, she stood-up, grabbed the milking jug, filled it with warm water, and handed it to her grandson. He, too, took it in silence and walked out of the kitchen, turned right, and headed straight for the stall. Once inside, he secured the cow in position by tying it with a halter to a sturdy post. He washed her udders and its hairless teats before milking. Grass tainted water crawled down his hands as the cow stood still to the warm massaging hands. Washing his hands, he took a clear milking jell and rubbed it gently onto the cow's teats. The cow mooed softly as his hands came in contact with its thick, hard slippery nipples. Bulging milk ducts protruded on the milk filled udders.

Agoyi took his milking stool and sat down with his legs spread apart. With his milk jar in his left hand, he wrapped his hand around cow's teats. He massaged it gently. The cow mooed and he began to squeeze its teats, firmly, steadily, and carefully. He dared not unsettle the cow. The cow stood still. A creamy-white substance gushed out of its teat cisterns falling into the jar with a loud splatter. It took him close to twenty minutes to complete this task.

When he finished, he untied the cow from its halter, pushed the door to the stall open and walked out all the way to the kitchen. He handed his grandmother the milk and walked out. The sun was already bright and warm, and it appeared unclouded and dazzling. He could feel its warmth as he headed back to his hut where he retreated. Impious thoughts of what lay ahead of him continued to trouble his mind. He collapsed on his chair in deep contemplation. Bright beams of light seeped into the house through the now wide-open window casting a translucent glow upon him. Suddenly, he felt warm inside. He did not move from his chair, but followed the light with his eyes all the way to the wall where it fell. He moved his eyes from the wall in a gradual manner, but still following the sun's rays through his pellucid window all the way to Maragoli hills. Misty fog on the hills had already evaporated. Instead, the sun's bright rays bedazzled the eastern hemisphere. Thoughts of his infinite possibilities of his future flashed through his mind. He contemplated telling the Oldman about the heist. Really! He did. If he did, he could redeem himself and probably have a future . . . Education. Yes! He could go back to school, study hard and make something out of his damned life. He could become a teacher. On second thought, he changed his mind about teaching. There was no money in teaching. No. He could become a doctor—a medical doctor—that is it. He could become a doctor. Better yet, he could become a chemist, work within a laboratory setting, developing a vaccine to cure AIDS or cancer. That would be noble. Yes. He had to consider seriously his future aspirations.

His thoughts floundered off course as dark grey clouds glided into the sun's path, casting upon it a temporary shadow. Agoyi remained soundless; his thoughts were still thwarted with his hopes and dreams: A good life. That was all there was to it . . .

When his grandmother called him for breakfast, he was still agonizing about his decision. He emerged from his hut in a drunken stupor, torn between his betrayal of his family and the good nature of his grandparents and the Haughty Boys' hooliganism. Even if he could see the world around him changing, he could not stop it. He, too, had changed, but lacked the gumption to acknowledge that truth. Even the security he had felt upon his entry into his grandparents' lives seemed to have dwindled rapidly when he joined hands with Kahuga. His sanctuary shattered like a boulder detached from Maragoli hills that tumbles to the riverbed fragmented into small pieces. No one, but himself, could intervene. Unfortunately, he had already formed a pact with the devil.

That morning, he ate in silence. When he finished, he thanked his grandmother and excused himself. He dared not linger there too long least they detect his sombre mood. He returned to his hut and reclined on his chair. He only had one chore to complete: to cut Napier grass for the cows. He could not do it too early because the ground was still saturated from the heavy rain.

While he was still resting peacefully, he heard a knock on his door. It was none other than Kahuga. His unexpected visitor made him feel even more uncomfortable.

"Quick, come in before *Guku* sees you," he said.

Kahuga was very jolly. There was a strange sparkle in his eyes. His unkempt hair snaked out of the hem of his red cap.

"I have something for you," he said as he stepped inside.

"Good! I could use some cheer about now."

"I know you are going to love it!" he said with a roguish grin on his face.

"Hope you are right."

"Of course am sure . . . I am always right!" Kahuga said braggingly.

"Let me see it!" Agoyi demanded.

Kahuga was in no hurry. He paraded the floor like a turkey. Beams of light fell on him as he walked in its path, casting his long narrow distorted shadow upon the wall. It vanished immediately he moved from its path.

"He did it!" Kahuga said gleefully.

"Who?"

"Chonjo! Who else? He did it man!"

"Really?" Agoyi exclaimed with disbelief. "That soon?"

"What did I tell you ha!? What did I tell you?"

Agoyi's eyes brightened to the good news, and his gloominess vanished. Reaching into his pocket, Kahuga pulled out a wad of notes and began to count: One, two— one hundred shilling notes, two twenty shilling notes, and finally six ten shilling notes; all mounting to three hundred shillings in total.

"You are kidding me right?" Agoyi said.

"No! I don't kid. Can you believe this?

"You rogue you!" Agoyi said.

Kahuga's delight and excitement erased most of Agoyi's uneasiness that had plagued him since dawn. He was his old self once again.

The boys split the money three ways, each boy receiving a hundred shillings . . . that was more money than Agoyi had ever held in his entire life time.

"If I didn't have one more chore, I'd have gone to buy something nice," Agoyi said.

"What do you have to do?"

"Cut grass!"

"I see!"

There was silence.

"I see," Kahuga said again. "Tell you what . . . If I help you, can we go out later?"

"Maybe!"

"No, not maybe. I need your word!"

"Okay! I have to ask my grandmother."

"It is settled then!"

"Sure . . . Let us go."

Though his grandmother disliked Kahuga, Agoyi hoped she would forgive him once she saw he had volunteered to help him. He was right. The boys walked together into the cowshed, took a *panga,* two sisal bags, and two ropes and ambled out. They passed the kitchen, passed the giant cemented water tank, and disappeared into the dense banana plantation towards the napier grass field. As they walked, Kahuga stepped on something. It was a round, soft and mushy. It busted open under his weight. He slipped nearly falling as his sole came in contact with its hard dark-brown seed. A pale green mushy mash spread on the sole of his foot oozing between his toes all the way to the edge of his foot. He cursed profusely, looking for a leaf to wipe the mash off his foot. Agoyi laughed at him in a hearty manner. Kahuga was in a good mood and was not offended.

"I don't think we should carry-on the heist tonight," Kahuga said after cleaning his foot.

"I thought you were set on tonight!"

"I was, but the ground is too saturated."

Agoyi sighed with relief.

"How will the others know of the change?"

"Don't worry, I will alert them."

"I see," Agoyi said.

The boys walked in silence until they reached the Oldman's napier grass field.

"Let us start here," Agoyi said.

"How far do you want us to go?"

"All the way to the school fence . . . That should be sufficient grass for the cows," Agoyi said, rolling-up his sleeves. Kahuga followed suit.

"Hand me the *panga*," Kahuga said.

"We'll take turns. You cut the grass while I pile it in heaps."

"Alright," Kahuga said getting to business and breaking into song:

My panga is sharp!

Yes, your panga is sharp

My panga was sharp

Yes, your panga was sharp

Kahuga whistled and Agoyi responded in whistle. The boys worked rhythmically to the sound of their voices and slashing of the *panga*. They changed their song as they continued with their task:

Woi the line

We have formed the line

Let us come together

We have formed the line

We have formed the line

Kahuga cut the grass; Agoyi picked and piled it in manageable heaps. When he got tired, they traded places. Agoyi cut the grass; Kahuga picked and piled it in even mounts.

By midday, the boys had finished cutting the grass. They tied each pile with a rope, carrying it back home. This took several trips. It was during their second trip that the boys bumped into Agoyi's grandmother. She gave Agoyi a mean look, but he was quick to say, "Kahuga agreed to help me with the grass."

"Uuh," she said gritting her teeth, but did not add anything further.

On their way back, the boys walked passed her, passed the water tank, and passed the avocado plant all the way to the field. The old lady watched them until their bodies were concealed by the napier grass. She walked inside the kitchen and began to prepare their lunch, grumbling: "Foolish boy!"

The boys continued with their work until they had finished carrying all the grass into the pen. That was not all. They chopped some of it, placed it in the trough, and released the cows for their morning feed. The only task Agoyi had left was to give the animals water, and that did not take much time. He had to wait until after lunch. Beyond that, he was free to rest during the afternoon. His grandmother did not reprimand him for keeping company with Kahuga, at least not on that day. When she served them lunch at noon, she thanked Kahuga for his service, but gave her grandson a meaningful gaze of displeasure. Agoyi understood the meaning of her stare

. . .

Chapter 23

On the night of the heist, it was impenetrably dark and the air was calm. Not even night-runners accustomed to nightly escapades could see through its density. That did not stop Haughty Boys. They were four in total, determined in their quest to reap havoc on their unsuspecting victim: the Oldman. He was one of the most respectable men from Ngoroke Village. This was the biggest sting of the year, and the boys knew it. They had coveted it ever since their formation, but had no way of completing it. That time dawned when Agoyi was coerced into joining the boys. The profit they would make from this little larceny was enormous.

When the boys arrived at the Oldman's entrance gate, they halted there inspecting their surroundings. Its large maroon steel gate stood a distance from the main house and faced the entrance to the Oldman's house. Regardless of that, they had to be careful, lest they be caught unaware. The gate was locked from inside. There was no padlock on it as customary because Agoyi had deliberately left it off as instructed by Kahuga. He promised him a hefty bonus. From the outside, there was a tiny opening where he thrust his hand in order to unfasten the latch. Kahuga, the mastermind of the whole operation, moved forward, pushed his hand through the small opening, and slowly started pulling the latch up-and-down, up-and-down. It squeaked. "Oops!" he gasped, his body breaking into a cold sweat. He pushed it down, then up and down again. He repeated this motion several times until the latch opened. He heaved a sigh of relief, rubbing his hands together. He wiped sweat off his brow. Gently, he pushed the door open. "Quick, get in!" he instructed the boys leading the way. Soundlessly, the boys tip-toed into the compound. He pushed the door back, but did not completely thrust its latch in place. One of the boys mumbled something about being afraid, but Kahuga hushed him.

The distance from the gate to the Oldman's house was about twenty metres. To the left, facing the main house stood Agoyi's shack. It was a small brick walled hut just like the Oldman's, but his was chipped in its corner.

"You," Kahuga ordered Chonjo. "Watch the backdoor." The Oldman's door was made of steel, just like his gate, and was strong enough to bar out would be intruders.

"No problem *bwana*," Chonjo said.

"And you," he told the other young man, who remained nameless. "You have the front door. . . If you hear anything or see any movement whatsoever, alert us! Is that clear?" The boys had to be extra careful to avoid detection.

"Yes boss," the boy said.

"Move! What are you waiting for?" Kahuga barked. Both boys hurried off, each heading to his post to keep a vigilant watch like an *askari*.

No sooner had the boys left than Kahuga made his way to Agoyi's shack. When he got there, he made a quick sweep of the compound with his eyes one more time. He did not see or hear anything. Certain no one was insight, he tapped lightly on the door. There was no sound. He tapped it again. There was no sound. Pressing his face on the cold metallic door, he whispered, "Agoyi! Are you in there?" Still, there was no answer. "Agoyi . . . Are you in there?" he said once more.

Then he heard a feeble voice from the inside say, "Is that you Kahuga?"

"Yeah, it is me! Hurry-up, will you."

He heard Agoyi turn the latch on his door slowly. There was silence, a clicking sound followed. He pulled the door open and walked out. As he emerged out of the hut into the open, he came face-to-face with Kahuga, but he could barely see him. His eyes were not accustomed to the dark. Cool air brushed against his brow, but unmoved by it; his heart throbbed with fear and agony of betrayal.

"Come on man! Let us go," Kahuga commanded. Agoyi tagged behind him like a puppy.

"How long do you suppose this job is going to take?"

"Probably a half an hour maximum . . . that is if all goes well," Kahuga said reassuringly.

In this manner, the prowlers embarked on their despicable plan.

When the boys reached the water tank, they agreed Kahuga would climb first followed by Agoyi. The tank was a humongous structure with thick cemented walls. It was not wet and produced no sound as the boys ascended it. Kahuga crawled-up the wall like a prowler trailed by his friend.

Once they were safely on the tank, Kahuga took the commanding lead. "Now, Agoyi, point the light here so I can see!" Agoyi flicked the switch of the torch to 'on.' He could now see the nails that were loosely hanging above the zinc sheet. "Move it closer!" he murmured. Agoyi did as he was instructed. Kahuga pried out the already loosened nails. He handed them to Agoyi for safe keeping or until they were ready to replace them.

No sooner had he pulled out the nails than he ordered again. "Hand me the light!"

"Here!" Agoyi said, handing him the spot light.

"Now, hold onto this zinc sheet. Once I get inside,

you can put it back in its place. Hop down, turn around the corner so you can help me."

"Alright then!"

Slowly, Kahuga lowered his body into the granary. When he was half-way down, he jumped inside, landing on a sack of maize making a puff-like sound. He did not move for a second listening. He did not hear a sound from inside the house. Without wasting time, he slowly opened the window. And with that, the robbery was on in full swing. The boys emptied the contents of the Oldman's granary, one scoop at a time. Kahuga scooped the grains; he handed it to Agoyi through the window, and he placed it in a container on the ground. The other two boys hauled it away. This went on for a long time; it was a prolonged and arduous endeavour. The boys worked ferociously, not even stopping to rest, and until they lost track of time, though timing was everything. Nevertheless, when they heard Irene's yelping, summoning the morning dawn, they knew they had to make haste, lest they be caught unaware.

Once he had finished, Kahuga locked the window and immediately found himself in a fix. He could not climb out of the granary. There was nothing he could use to get out, not even a sack of maize. The only thing left outside the room were empty shelves, but they were too far for his reach. This was a minor complication he had not foreseen. Befuddled, he started pacing the floor, mumbling "What to do! What to do!"

Suddenly, he remembered a story his grandmother had once told him. It was a story about the cunning hare. In his mind's eye, her voice was as clear as the very day she had told him the story. "Once upon a time, there lived Hare and his grandmother. She was too old to until her land. When planting season came, Hare lied to her: 'I have already grown our crops.' Every morning, he worked the farm. When the weeding season came, he left home at dawn and returned at dusk. When harvest time came, he left home in the morning and returned at night with his harvest. Hare would creep into other farmers' gardens at night and steal their groundnuts.

One day, one of the farmers was so angry that someone was stealing his groundnuts that he decided to set a trap to catch the thief. The farmer made a beautiful scarecrow out of glue. He put a scarecrow into his garden that evening, and then he went off to bed. That night, the lazy and cunning hare decided to steal some more groundnuts from the farmer's garden. Hare snuck into the farmer's garden and made his way towards the groundnuts. Then, he saw the scarecrow. He became mesmerized by her beauty that he walked over to talk to her. 'Hello,' he said, blushing slightly, 'You are very beautiful. Will you shake my hand?'

Hare put out his hand and grasped the beautiful scarecrow's hand, but scarecrow's hand was made from glue. Hare's hand got stuck. 'Let me go!' he cried, trying to pull away. 'Let me go or I'll hit you!' he shouted. Nothing Happened. He slapped the scarecrow with his free hand, but it, too, got stuck!

Hare tried to kick the scarecrow, but his foot got stuck. Next, he tried to stamp with her foot, and his other foot got stuck too. This way, the lazy hare was stuck to the scarecrow. There was nothing he could do, but wait. The next morning, the farmer came down to his garden and saw hare stuck on the scarecrow. 'So it was you who was stealing my groundnuts!' he roared. He pried hare from the scarecrow and tucked him under his arm. 'I'll teach you a lesson for stealing from me,' the farmer growled. 'I'll cook you in my pot and eat you all up.'

Agoyi's grandmother's voice faded to Irene's voice as she summoned the dawn:

Kindu cha ndanyoola ne ling'ana

Luuya

Kindu cha ndanyoola ne ling'ana

  Luuya

"Agoyi!" he growled. "I am stuck in here . . . I can't come out."

"Why is that?"

"I have nothing to use to climb out."

"I have a great idea!"

"What?"

"Just wait in there for a minute. I will be right back."

"Hurry-up, will you?"

"Be right back," Agoyi said as he disembarked the tank. He ran into the pen and returned with a rope.

Quickly, he mounted the tank.

"Okay Kahuga . . . I am back!" He tied the rope tightly around his right hand. Using his left hand, he lowered it into the granary. He held it hard with stiffened arms. "Now, grab onto it tightly. Tell me when you are ready."

 "Now!"

Agoyi started to pull-out his odd cargo. He could hear Kahuga's huffing and puffing as he tried to heave his body up to the wall like a cat. Suddenly, the unexpected happened. The rope snapped, breaking into two pieces. Kahuga tumbled backwards, landing on the hard cold surface with an awful thump. "Ouch!" he squealed as a shockwave of pain crawled up his spine. His red cap fell off, but he was too distracted by pain to notice. Even Agoyi nearly fell into the granary, but he held tightly onto the rim of the tank.

"Are you okay in there?" he whispered.

"Yeah right!" he said sarcastically. "Just get me out of here please."

Agoyi pulled the rope out, folded it in half, pulled on it to test its strength, and then lowered it to him again.

Kahuga grabbed onto it tightly. "Now!" he yelled. Agoyi lugged forward, pulling Kahuga out of his jam. As he got out, his entire body was dabbed in sweat, but relieved to be out; after all, he was no hare. Once outside, he handed Agoyi the light and replaced the roof top, ensuring the nails were securely fastened. The boys hopped off the tank and assisted the other boys in hauling everything they had to Kahuga's home. From there, they would sell it to anyone who wanted it for a profit. "What a perfect job!" the boys bragged to themselves. The operation was a successful heist—one clean heist. No near capture experience . . . Little did they know that the days of a thief are numbered . . . Only theirs came sooner than they had anticipated.

Chapter 24

The next morning was the first Sunday in January, and Agoyi had a slow start to his day. He was so exhausted from his previous night's escapades that he did not hear the end of Irene's dawn singing, which he used as his alarm. He was startled from his sleep by his grandmother's loud banging at his door.

"Agoyi," she called.

There was no answer.

"Agoyi!" she called and followed it by a loud banging sound on the door.

Again, there was no answer.

After several unanswered successive knocks, the old woman walked back to her kitchen puzzled. This was the first time Agoyi had been unable to wake-up on time to milk the cows.

Rattled from his sleep by the loud knock, Agoyi staggered out of his bed, tossing his covers to its lower end. He did not make his bed, promising to return later for a quick catnap. He raced into the kitchen only to find his grandmother had already warmed the water he needed for milking.

"I am sorry *Guku* for being late," he said apologetically.

"Don't worry my child. Am glad to know you are alright," she said.

"Am sorry," he said again, taking the jar of warm water.

He walked out of the kitchen, embarking on his task right away. He completed his chores expediently, ate his breakfast, and excused himself. He marched back to his hut and went back to sleep.

Nothing happened that day . . .

Two days came and passed. Still nothing happened. For two successive nights, the boys met at the summit. They seldom talked about the heist save for how to dispose of their loot. It was not difficult at all. On the third day, there were some interested party. On the fifth day many people willing to freely give the boys money for their merchandise, which they sold at a throw-away price. Hardly anyone bothered to ask the boys how they had come into possession of their merchandise. This was not surprising. Chonjo, the Dispatcher, who was the face of the operation, would have answered any question. He was an astute business man. He was very crafty. He also had a very sweet tongue, a quality which made him ideal for his many assignments. He could sell anything in his possession in a jiffy, even if it was worthless. He looked into his customer's eyes with an unflinching gaze, staring the person into submission. With a charming smile, he baited his customer in this manner. If it was a woman, he would say, *"Look here mama! Look at this! Have you ever seen anything as good as this maize? If you don't believe, just feel it. This maize is the best. It is clean, as clean as it gets—no stones in it, no weevils. I checked it myself! . . . Tell you what, if you buy it from me, I will even carry it for you to your destination. If you don't like it, let me know when you see me next time,"* but that never happened, at least not yet. If a customer did not want to buy anything, he would move on, looking for another gullible client whom he would trick into spending his or her last penny. Such was the case when Chonjo, the Dispatcher dispatched the grain they stole from Keya and the loot from the Oldman's home . . .

On the sixth day following the heist, Agoyi awoke to startling mournful shrieks. It was the sound of his grandmother's voice. He jumped out of bed, worried something bad may have happened to the Oldman. He pushed his door wide open and roughly slammed it back in place. The door rattled, but he did not look back. He sprinted towards the wailing sound of his grandmother, passed the kitchen, passed the cemented water tank, all the way to the back door. The door was open, and she was sitting sombrely on the steps. The door to her storage was wide open, and he could tell it had been swept clean. Her chest was heaving rapidly. Warm tears streamed out of her eyes. She kept on saying: "Why! Why!"

The sorrowful sight of his grandmother saddened him very much. He almost collapsed as his feet jelled from under him and his heart began to pound hard and loud. Leaning on the wall, he staggered towards her. The truth was out finally, and he was devastated by it just as much as his grandmother.

The Oldman, like his grandson, hearing his wife's wailing, raced toward the back of the house. He found the duo looking glum. When he saw the emptiness of his store, he understood the reason for his wife's wailing. They had been robbed, and he did not hear it. This truth nearly gave the Oldman a heart attack.

"Was the door open when you got here," he asked.

"No!" she said.

"How about the window . . . was it open?"

"That is just the problem! It wasn't."

"How do you suppose they got in?"

"That's what I have been thinking about all this time!"

"How come we didn't hear them?" he asked.

"I don't know! . . . I couldn't tell you," she said. "They must have used some potent magic to lull us into sleep," she added. "Yes, we must have slept deep as death on the night of the robbery."

"You think so?"

"Maybe . . . No, it has to be so!"

The Oldman walked into the storage for inspection. There was nothing. He saw nothing. There was no sign of forced entry. The latch on his window was not broken. There was no scratch on the back door or the window. He could not explain it. He could not explain the mystery behind the robbery. Maybe his wife was right. The thieves must have used powerful magic to break into their home. That had to be it.

Without saying a word, he walked out of the storage, leaving Agoyi and his wife behind. He did not tell them where he was going or what he was about to do. Minutes later, he returned with Iliigutu. He, too, after close inspection of the site simply said: "What a clever job." He, like the Oldman, inspected the scene after the crime, but was equally befuddled, bamboozled, and stupefied by it.

"You said you didn't hear anything?"

"Not even a sound," the Oldman assured him.

"When was the last time you were in this room?"

"A week ago," the Oldman said. "Would you like to come in and talk? There is nothing we can do here."

"Certainly!"

The two men walked out and went back to the Oldman's living room. There, they remained for a very long time. Thinking and talking about how best to handle the matter at hand. Later, when the two men emerged from the house, they decided *Iliigutu* would launch an inquest into the robbery. But without any evidence, it was a lost cause.

When word went out about the robbery at the Oldman's home, not a single man or woman acknowledged any knowledge of the robbery. Everyone was shocked. The superstitious ones believed magic had everything to do with it. Those who hated the Oldman simply said, "It served him right!"

As clean as the heist was, the Divine hands of Providence had a way of coming to the rescue of those victimized by impious men. A week passed. Nothing happened. Two weeks passed. Nothing happened. Three weeks, but still nothing happened. People had even begun to forget the Oldman, and his wife had been robbed. Hardly anyone talked about Keya and Desi's robbery; their's only was a speck in the depth of this grandiose universe. People did not make much of it. Nevertheless, the Oldman's heist had drawn everyone's ear and attention, just as Kahuga had predicted, a prelude to a good storytelling . . .

When the late January rains came, most people began to ready themselves for the planting season. Those without seedlings purchased them from Kenya Cereal Board or a reputable shop. Those who could not afford a purchase soaked their *kebeedi* maize they had saved from the previous harvest. Although the Oldman had lost everything, his seedlings included, he managed to purchase enough for the planting season. When it was time, he planted his crops judiciously and on time as he always did.

By then, the boys had disposed of all their merchandise and shared their spoils . . . What a perfect job. But, as the proverbial expression goes '*Siku za mwizi ni arobaini';* the boys' day of reckoning was about to come, much sooner than they had anticipated and in a most unusual way.

One day, a neighbour appeared at *Iliigutu's* home, complaining about his crops which had dried-up unexpectedly after sprouting.

"Perhaps the soil was too saturated," *Iliigutu* told the man.

"I didn't think so!" the man protested.

"Perhaps you used too much fertilizer."

"You may have a point, but I doubt it."

The man returned to his home with a heavy heart. *Iliigutu* did not make much of the incident. He dismissed the man's call to be a casual neighbourly visit. Such conversations were not uncommon during any given planting season.

Within a day or so, a second man visited the man of the law. He, too, had a similar story. A third one came and a fourth; they all had the same story. This was the first time in the entire Ngoroke Village where poor farmers' crops had dried-up unexpectedly, even if the ground was not too saturated. 'Was this coincidental? These cases . . . It could be! No!' Iliigutu wondered. Right away, he began to suspect there was something more sinister about the men's stories than just a mere coincidence of their dried crops. His farm was not affected. There was no drought to justify the recounted events. The earth was saturated, but not too wet to cause the alleged destruction. It was ideal for new crops. He could touch it. He could feel it. He could smell it. It was moist, ideal for planting.

When a fifth man paid *Iliigutu* a visit, he listened to his tale sombrely and without interruption. "If his crops had dried naturally," he thought. "Why had he sought after him . . . No, there was something odd about it." This thought bothered him again and again and again. Finally, he asked the man, "What did you do differently when you planted your crops this year?"

The man sat quietly for a while, racking his brains. *Iliigutu* watched him out of the corner of his eyes. The man's eyes gazed emptily on the mud walls of Iliigutu's house. The man stood up and paced the room in a circular manner. Suddenly, as though struck with lightening, he began to bubble off:

"I remember it now! I remember it now! Yes, I remember it now."

Iliigutu's body stiffened. He lifted his head and faced the man. "Remember what?"

"What I did," the man said dropping his head in shame. "Don't judge me here," he added, a serious look appearing on his visage.

"I promise not to judge you! Just tell me what happened. What did you do differently this year?"

"Remember when the Oldman was robbed?"

"Oh no! You didn't have anything to do with it?" *Iliigutu* said as his eyes popped open. A bad thought cropped on his mind, *'I will kill him if he says he did it. So help me God!'*

"No. I had nothing to do with it."

"I see," a relieved, *Iliigutu* said, not convinced of the man's innocence.

"Now tell me what happened . . . everything that happened."

"This boy!"

"What boy?"

"He calls himself Chonjo, the Dispatcher."

"What did that scoundrel do this time?"

"He sold me this fertilizer he got from his brother."

"Which brother of his?"

"The one who works for the Cereal Board."

"Why would he do that?"

"I don't know. He told me he needed the money."

"And you believed him?"

"Of course!"

"And when was that?"

"Around the same time the Oldman was robbed."

"What did he tell you about it?"

"It was supposed to make my maize grow tall and strong."

"And you believed him?"

"Totally. My harvest is always poor. He promised me my harvest will surpass everyone in the village if I used it this year."

"Continue!"

"Who wouldn't have wanted to have a good crop? I bought the fertilizer without thinking. Now, I have nothing. My entire crop has been destroyed."

"Are you sure the boy got the fertilizer from his brother?"

"I had no reason to doubt him," the man said, dropping his eyes to the ground.

"I would not be surprised if the fertilizer you bought was stolen from the Oldman's house?"

"I wouldn't know about that . . . That boy convinced me he had got *it* from his brother. He even gave me tips on how to *properly* use it."

"What did he tell you?"

"He said I should sprinkle it around the stems of my crop after sprouting, which I did. Days after that, all my crops dried-up!"

"Are you serious?"

"If you do not believe me, come and see it for yourself."

The man of the law agreed to bear witness to the bizarre story. He followed the man all the way to his farm. Sure enough, his entire farm had the semblance of death, crop death that is—there was hardly any plant left standing. Everything had withered off. . .

Later that day, *Iliigutu* visited the Oldman. It was late in the afternoon and the Oldman had reclined on his chair under the canopy of his gum tree as he always did. The air was cool and soothing. His eyes were shut.

When *Iliigutu* arrived, he startled the Oldman from his nap with a greeting:

"How are you my friend?"

The Oldman, who was dozing off, grumpily mumbled, "What is it?"

"That is not the way to greet a friend," *Iliigutu* joked.

"Agoyi," the Oldman called out.

"Yes, *Guga,*" he said from inside the house.

"Could you bring me chair?"

"Yes, *Guga,*" he said. Hurriedly, Agoyi emerged with the chair. Greeted the man of the law and walked back into the house.

"He is a good boy," *Iliigutu* made an observation.

"Yes! He is not a bad boy. He is very helpful around here, especially looking after the cows. Bless his soul!"

"We need more young men like him in this village."

"You are right about that. There are many young men here who are very bad—like Kahuga and Chonjo. Or Kabwoni!"

"Don't mention that fool. He beat his father Kaduma over a piece of land."

"Didn't they say he broke his ribs?"

"Yes he did, but Kaduma was so stubborn," *Iliigutu* said with a giggle.

"I heard they had to drag him to the hospital."

"Thank God he didn't die of his injury."

"That would have been a big taboo in our village. The world has changed very much from our days."

"True!"

"Listen Mzee, I didn't come here to talk about the riff-raff in this village. Something happened this morning," *Iliigutu* said.

"What is it?" the Oldman said with a curious interest.

"Am not so sure," he paused. "Several farmers have been coming in to see me . . . There have been some developments regarding your stolen property."

"My case? After this long?"

"Am not sure, but numerous farmers have been in to see me."

"What about?"

"They have been complaining about their withered crops. . . Have you had any problems with your crop?"

"No. My crop is fine. Nothing out of the ordinary has happened."

Iliigutu reclined in his chair, like the Oldman, and closed his eyes.

"May I look at that room again—I mean, the storage," *Iliigutu* said.

"Sure. I don't know what you hope to find. I haven't been in there. Not even my wife," the Oldman said.

The two men walked back to the backdoor of his house, pushed the door open and walked into the storage. It was dark and empty. The Oldman walked toward the window and pushed its latch to the right. It clicked as the window fell open. A cool draft swept the entire room. Bright streaming light exposed the bareness of the room. A thick lump cropped in the Oldman's throat. He sighed despairingly, "too many bad memories," he noted.

Iliigutu began to inspect the room closely; something he failed to do day the robbery was exposed. He moved from one corner to another. It was during that time he saw a red object sandwiched between shelves on the right-side corner of the storage. Without a word, he walked toward the corner, pushed his hand between the shelves and pulled it out. It was a crumpled red cap.

"Do you know who this belongs to?" he asked the Oldman.

"No!" he said. "But it looks familiar," he paused. "I am not sure," the Oldman added. "I just can't recollect, but I know I have seen it."

The men walked backed to the tree shade and there, they remained for a very long time, nagged by the red cap. It was at that time *Iliigutu* learned that among the things which had been stolen from the Oldman's storage was a half-full sack of fertilizer. It was a type he only used on his tea plants. Everything made sense now. The men whose crops had withered might have bought fertilizer from the same source, Chonjo, the Dispatcher.

"The boy has to know something," *Iliigutu* said.

Excusing himself, *Iliigutu* went straight to the last man whom he had spoken to earlier that morning. Both men walked to Chonjo's home. As soon as the boy saw them, with the red cap in the elder's hand, he knew something was wrong. *Iliigutu* does not visit people's homes without reason. Immediately, he started running . . . And running he did.

The chase was on. The men ran after him.

"*Huyo mshike*—Catch him!" *Iliigutu* yelled.

There was no one close by to help them. The boy ran with cheetah speed. Being old, they were no match for him. Chonjo was a good sprinter, which worked to his advantage. He disappeared out of their view, and hide behind the crevices in the rocks. He knew his terrain well enough to evade capture for several hours.

Unable to locate him, the men returned to his home and left word that were he to return, he should be detained.

It was obvious Chonjo had not worked alone. Had they captured him, he would have led them to his accomplice. The rumour about the boy's misdeeds spread fast. There was also the issue of the red cap. It was not difficult to link it to its owner, Kahuga. He was the only person in Ngoroke village who always wore a red cap. To lure him to his capture, *Iliigutu* sent someone to his grandparents' home. The man deceived him into thinking he had found his cap on the road, but had forgotten it at his home. If he wanted it, he could go to the *Baraza* for it.

Poor boy, he fell into the trap, for he had not remembered where he lost it. When he got to the *Baraza*, he found *Iliigutu* there waiting for him. He had no way of escaping. He had fallen into the trap like the hare who had beguiled his grandmother. Kahuga had become stuck on the *scarecrow* of his hat.

When he was interrogated, he named all his co-conspirators, but not without the coaxing of a whip. He named them all, including Agoyi.

"You are lying boy!" *Iliigutu* said harshly and in disbelief.

"I am not," he said. *Iliigutu* would not hear it. He gave the boy a fierce lash on his left cheek.

"Tell me the truth boy!"

"It is the truth!"

"What do you know about truth?"

"It is!" Sadly, he neglected to say was how he had blackmailed Agoyi into robbing his own grandfather.

"That boy has more sense in him than ten of you. He couldn't do a thing like that to his own folks!" he added, giving Kahuga another fierce lash.

"If you don't believe me, ask him."

"I plan to!" *Iliigutu* said.

The boy fell down on the ground face down writhing in pain, but he was not sorry he had done it. "I should have been careful," he mumbled.

"Bring Agoyi here," he barked.

A timid Agoyi was manhandled to the man of the law. Not once did he look at Kahuga.

"Did you have anything to do with this?" he queried, with a crackle in his voice.

Agoyi was silent.

"Did you? Speak-up boy, or else," *Iliigutu* said, raising his hand-up to slap the boy.

"Tell him!" Kahuga said in a vengeful voice.

Agoyi looked at him with angry eyes. *Iliigutu* whacked him across his face.

"Speak-up boy!" *Iliigutu* barked at him.

"Yeees!" he said with a slight sniffle.

"Yes, what?"

"Yes, *Iliigutu*. I took part in the robbery," breaking down in tears, ashamed of his actions.

As he stood before the man of the law, watching his world crumple, his mind took flight to the first day he had seen Kahuga. He recollected his grandmother's warning: *"That boy . . . he is one of the most imprudent and ill-natured boys in the entire village. I don't want you near him. Do you understand? You must avoid him like one avoids a leper. . . He is a cancer. You must avoid him no matter what!"*

Iliigutu gave him another whipping, but he felt no pain. He just stood there, emotionless, and taking his punishment like a man and without protest.

As for the Oldman, he was bamboozled by his grandson's behaviour. He quietly wondered why he had not suspected him. His wife was heartbroken and that was all there was to it.

"Once you are done with him," the Oldman told *Iliigutu* . . . "the boy needs to be returned to his father." He could not speak any more . . .

By the day's end, all the four boys had been rounded and were in *Iliigutu's* custody at the *Baraza.* The police had been called in order to take them to the station for further interrogation. Most Ngorokeans were astounded by the sad spectacle. Some, especially those guilty by association, stood on the peripheral watching the unfolding drama. Their eyes were cowed in cowardice as though afraid of being implicated in the unfortunate fiasco. They, too, deserved to be incarcerated alongside the boys. Others, whose crops had dried-up, the Divine hands of Providence had already dealt them the ultimate verdict: A dead harvest. The story of Haughty Boys, like that of Jumba who had killed his cousin Asah and buried him in his compound, became immortalized in the lore of Ngoroke people, just as Kahuga had predicted . . .

Chapter 25

When the police arrived at the *Baraza*, the sun was now below the horizon, leaving a few faint streaks of red on the western sky. And the air was fresh and cool. Immediately, the police hauled the boys like sacks and tossed them into the back of the Landrover. Kahuga's red cap fell to the ground. He did not bend to pick it, only a faint smile of triumph appeared across his face. Agoyi's swollen red eyes darted furtively behind his eyebrows. His bruised hands were firmly held together with handcuffs. On his cheeks, double thin moist streams glided like the Buhani River. His chest heaved rapidly with a maddening rage. No. It was not a maddening rage. It was an emotional pain, of the loss of his father's trust, of the loss of the Oldman and his grandmother that had meant the world to him. It was an emotional loss all right. That fateful evening, his mind, wrung like a wet towel, seethed with a wrath of a family betrayed. Deep down his soul, he knew and bore ownership of the tragic events of his life. He could not blame anyone else, but himself. Beyond that, he was flittingly bedevilled with the image of his long deceased mother. It appeared and vanished from his mind at the click of the ignition of the Landrover. His misty eyes struggled to peer through the dusty pellucid windshield, gaping at the Oldman whose hands were firmly pressed on his waist. Their eyes met. And just for a fraction of a second, he wanted to say: "Please forgive me," but it was too late. The driver had already pressed hard on the gas pedal. All he could hear now was the sound of tires grinding on the gravel road as the Landrover sped towards the Police station, leaving behind swirling dust and a crushed red cap. The Oldman followed the Landrover with his eyes until its shape was no more than a brown dot at the far end to the village obscured by a trail of swirling dust . . .

Days, weeks, months, and even years following the Haughty Boys' arrest, their purloining habits exposed, Ngorokeans spoke of their unruliness as unforgettable lessons. Those with young children warned them of the perils of joining gangs: *"You don't want to end-up like Haughty Boys: Behind bars. If you have any sense left in you, listen to your elders by amending your ways."*

The elders vowed never to be beguiled by those whose tongues are as sweet as nectar, for behind the sweetness, there might be a lurking devil ready to lure weak unconscionable souls . . .

www.ingramcontent.com/pod-product-compliance
Lightning Source LLC
Chambersburg PA
CBHW020230030726
47497CB00009B/3029